LET'S LIVE AGAIN

LET'S LIVE AGAIN

NISHA PARYANI SHARMA

PARTRIDGE
A Penguin Random House Company

To order additional copies of this book, contact
Partridge India
000 800 10062 62
www.partridgepublishing.com/india
orders.india@partridgepublishing.com

CONTENTS

DEDICATED TO

My husband for putting his valuable inputs,
my grandparents for their great love, my parents for
their endless support and making me worth of what I am
today, my bhaiya and bhabhi for giving me unrelenting
passion to reach my goal and my loving family who
always stand beside me.

ACKNOWLEDGEMENTS

I express my deep gratitude towards:

- ❖ My publisher Partridge Publishing Services who had helped me throughout the editing, production and publishing process to fulfill my dream of my book at its best.
- ❖ My parents for imbibing in me all the values.
- ❖ My in-laws family to support me at every stage.
- ❖ My friends who had always encouraged me.
- ❖ My GOD who had given me everything what I wanted.

1st Meeting

Knock Knock

"Please come in," Nysha maam said.

"Hii! This is Rajveer Ranawat, sorry for coming late, actually I got stuck in traffic. You know how Delhi traffic is?" Rajveer said while entering in the office and putting forward his right hand for a hand shakes.

Rajveer Ranawat, looked like a bollywod hero, tall, quite fair and handsome with a lean body. He was wearing dark blue jeans and white shirt, white adidas shoes and a classy watch; must be of some international brand. His eyes were black, rough hairs with a little beard on his face. I was wondering how come such a smart guy needs to meet Nysha maam.

"Hello Rajveer! I am Nysha, Please have a seat." Nysha maam said while shaking hand with a pleasing smile and indicated him to sit on the chair placed in front of her desk.

OMG! What to say about Nysha maam. She is so beautiful, so energized and so pleasing that once by looking at her no one could believe that she is at age of 45. She was wearing white and pink chudidaar kurta, her shoulder length hairs were open and front layer was clutched by 2 pins on the right side of head. Her face was shining as always and her lips were twinkling because of the gloss she'd applied.

"So Rajveer, how is everything going?" Nysha maam said with a tender smile.

"Nothing is fine Nysha Ji, that's why I'm sitting over here with you," Rajveer answered while looking all around Nysha maam's office.

In front of the office door was Nysha maam's desk with her rotating chair at one side and 2 such chairs on the other side. Her desk was so clean with only a laptop at one side and a notepad, pen stand with 5-6 coloured pens and pencils and small family photograph placed on the other side of the desk facing her. On the right side of desk was a large glass window beside which there was a sofa set and a center table with some magazines kept over it.

Dark brown curtains with floral print were looking so good on side of the glass windows. Through the window one can see the nice view of city. At one corner there was a big vase with fresh roses. Nysha maam had a habit of changing the roses daily when she enters in the room.

"Ok so tell me what is not fine with you? What is it that is bothering you?" Nysha maam said softly while looking into the eyes of Rajveer.

"I don't know. I actually don't know. It seems as if I am completely lost. I'm not me. This is not me. Just look at me An Empty Idiot Box," Rajveer said in a low tone initially which turned into depressive tone.

"Just relax Rajveer, do you need some water?" Nysha maam asked while offering a glass of water placed on her desk, Nysha maam continued and this time she stood from her chair and started moving around Rajveer. "Alright tell me something about yourself, your likes, dislikes, your daily routine, your hobbies, friends, family. Tell me about it."

"I'm the only son of my parents or rather I should call 2 fighters of our house, my mom and dad fights brutally daily, their harsh noises are still running in my ears. I work in an MNC and I just hate it when my boss barks on me for targets, sales and performance. I love to be with my friends who are now all far away and got busy with their lives and family. Last month was my girlfriend's marriage and she flew away to Australia. I hate that bitch that dumped me for an NRI. And now I don't feel like doing anything. I feel exhausted and completely lost, since for the past 8 months I'm just moving; but where and why I don't know," Rajveer said almost crying in one continuous tone and stopped to get a breathe and drank the glass of water in one gulp.

After a pause he continued, "2 days back I saw your advertisement in newspaper and now I'm here. I need your help. Will you please help me out?"

"Of course I will!! I guess that's why I'm here," Nysha maam said righteously putting her hand on Rajveer's shoulder.

And they continued for talking about half an hour and Rajveer was illustrating himself to get understood but I was more concentrated on Nysha maam. Just look at her, so simple yet so elegant and the most wonderful part is her pleasant smile. During the whole conversation she was constantly smiling and listening carefully to Rajveer. And at last their next meeting was fixed for tomorrow 5 in the evening.

Her smile made me remind of the proverb, "Your smile is the door to enter in someone's heart," and this is it Nysha maam's smile had allowed her to enter in my heart.

CHAPTER 1

Smile Please

L et me first begin with by asking you some simple questions. Do you like a crying baby or the one who always smile? Do you like a lethargic and tired boy who always complain or the one who is always energetic, enthusiastic and make you laugh with his jokes? Do you like the receptionist at the counter giving you annoyed looks or the one who greets you wih the smile?

If I'm not wrong you must have chosen the second option of each question; isn't it? Can you guess, what is the similarity between all the answers which you had choosen? Yes!! You have rightly figured it out. It's SMILE.

Smile is the entrance gate to enter in someone's heart. Every day we met with many people but we get attracted to someone who gives us a pleasing smile and for courtesy we also smile back. Have you ever thought why do people smile when they greet each other? It's because while smiling, our heart opens the door for new ideas, new people, new life, and new energy to come inside us and fills us with joy and happiness. Whenever we see a small child, we use to try all our best efforts just to see him smiling because according to me a baby's smile create a vibration in our body and fills us with so much charismatic energy and we tend to forget our surrounding environment and we just be the way what we are and start playing with the kid, talking with him in an uncertain tone and start doing all actions just to make that kid smile and after sometime if we observe ourselves, huge amount of radiant energy is coming out from us and we create an aura of that happiness, joy and energy around us.

> *"A smile is a curve that sets everything straight."*
> —*Phyllis Diller*

Welcome every morning with a smile. Look on the new day as another special gift from your Creator, another golden opportunity to complete what you were unable to finish yesterday. Be a self starter. Let you first set the theme of success and positive action that is certain to echo through your entire day. Today will never happen again. Don't waste it with a false start or no start at all. Begin your day with a pleasing smile.

In our childhood we have been going to circus with our parents and the very one thing which attracts us is JOKER. He wears such colourful dress, make different faces still we like him because he always smile and also puts all his efforts to make us smile. As it is said one is not fully dressed until he wears a smile. And that joker's smile is the shortest distance between you and him. Once he smiles, you stay connected to him. That joker's smile also gives us a message that:

Smile; don't frown.
Look up; don't look down.
Believe in yourself; don't let yourself go.
Just be who you are; and let your life flow.

Smile is God's gift to us and we should be thankful to God that he had given us a life in which by just smiling we can keep our soul happy and give a charming expression to whoever we meet. As according to Giblin Les, "If you're not using your smile, you're like a man with a million dollars in the bank with no cheque book."

Whenever you go to a photo studio, you do all preparation. You wear the best dress, best shoes, best make up, best hair style so that you look best but you're not fully dressed until you wear a smile. That one moment of smile creates a beautiful picture and its memory lasts forever. So imagine how your world will be if you start your day with a wonderful smile. Your smile will give you a positive countenance that will make people feel comfortable around you.

> *"Smile is an inexpensive way to change your looks."*
> —*Charles Gordy*

At last I would only say that smile brings rest to the weary, cheer to the discouraged, sunshine to the sad and it is nature's best antidote for trouble. And always follow Doug Horton rule which says, "Smile, it's a free therapy."

Make a promise to yourself that you'll start your day with a smile and end it with a smile, you give smile to every person you meet today let it be your mother, friend, neighbor, teacher, shopkeeper, doctor, vendor boy, your boss, colleague, customer, old lady, your classmate whoever it may be, spread your smile as you can; thinking as if you are spreading happiness around you.

2nd Meeting

It's already 20 past 5. I wondered Rajveer is still not there. I know he must have the same reason for coming late, "Traffic Jam."

Tring Tring

"Yes Nancy," Nysha maam said.

"Maam Mr. Rajveer is waiting outside," the receptionist of Nysha maam's office said.

"Tell him to wait for few more minutes while I get free from Mr. Bakshi (client sitting inside)," she replied and hung up the phone.

After 20 minutes.

"Good evening Nysha Ji, sorry for coming late, traffic jam you know!" Rajveer said dramatically while entering into the office room.

I just knew he will say such silly reason only.

"Very Good Evening Rajveer," Nysha maam greeted back with a smile and solicit him to have a seat.

"So, how was your day?" she asked.

"The day was boring as I did nothing. I was just sitting idle at home; wondering about what all is happening to me?" Rajveer said in a low tone.

"What is happening with you?" Nysha maam enquired.

"I don't know. Although I was sitting idle; I have nothing great to do still I'm feeling stressed out," Rajveer answered.

"Stress." She said while taking a deep breath. "Stress is not only due to physical work but is also because of mental pressure too."

Mental pressure? A sudden question came up in my mind and guess what Rajveer asked the same one, "Mental Pressure?" putting stress on these two words.

"Yes. Thinking too much about unwanted and negative thoughts, feeling which cause sadness or fill us with boredom causes mental pressure," she said and further put in plain words, "Our brain is like a machine which works 24*7 and just as a machine needs good oiling; the same goes for our brain. If we feed our brain with negative thoughts or redundant concern or unsubstantiated issues, our brain nerves got stuck and ultimately cause mental pressure."

"Do you mean my brain nerves are getting stuck?" Rajveer asked as he got interested in what Nysha maam was explaining.

"If you continue thinking like this; then YES may be," she said.

"O God! What am I doing to myself? I think I'll have a brain hemorrhage if I continue doing like this," Rajveer uttered to himself but audible enough to Nysha maam.

She consoled Rajveer and said, "Don't worry Rajveer. Nothing will happen to you. Stress is not that bad too."

Now I too have a question. Is Nysha maam playing a game or what? Tell me clearly whether stress is good or not; my mind was asking.

"Stress is not bad?? But right now you've just said it'll squeeze my brain nerves," Rajveer asked in sheer confusion.

"Don't get confused Rajveer; I'll make you clear of this," Nysha maam said with a smile as grinning as unnoticed.

"Anything within a limit is good for us but when it goes beyond that outer limit; it can be dangerous and harmful. And the same goes for stress too," she elucidate.

"Dangerous? So am I in a safe zone or a danger zone?" Rajveer asked and this time he got erect on his seat with back straight and leaning towards the desk to get an answer for his question and solve the query which was going on in his mind.

"You're on the edge of safe zone which if not controlled; you might get into the danger zone," she said while showing gestures with her 2 hands to make the two zones understood.

Tell me clearly whether stress is good or not; my mind was asking again.

"Nysha maam! It's because of the stress I've reached to the edge of safe zone and getting into the danger zone; then how could it be good?" Rajveer perplexed.

"Rajveer. It's because of stressss (putting pressure on the word stress) you're here," she said.

"I'm not getting it," Rajveer said in distress; leaning back to the chair.

"Now listen to me. It was the stress that brought you over here for a solution. If the stress level had exceeded its limit; you might be sitting in one of the hospital", she continued after a pause "stress is good for you as it pinpoints your head to get a solution over your troubles."

"You are trapped in your problems, feeling tensed about everything, thought of every negative feeling which causes mental pressure resulted in stress and because of all this stuff today you are sitting in front of me," she clarified.

Now I was calculating my stress level and getting to know where was I standing; safe zone or danger zone?

"Problems do come in our life and it will always come but what we need to do is change our response over it. A good thing about you is you'd at least taken an initiative to get the solution for your problem. So Mr. Rajveer, did you get my point?" she said with a cute smile.

"Yes Nysha Ji! I got it. You know I've read the definition of management in my MBA course which fits here very well and it says, "Optimum utilization of resources to get the maximum benefits" which means I've to get the maximum benefits of my optimum level of stress which is actually good for me," Rajveer said with a sigh of relief.

"Very well said Rajveer. Now you've got my point."

I also got my answer, my mind was saying. And the good thing was I was in a safe zone.

Later casual talks went over and the next meeting was fixed on Sunday.

CHAPTER 2

Little Stress is Necessary

We've often heard that partying with friends, drinking and eating chocolate in moderation can be good for you, now it seems that a little stress may be beneficial, too. We often heard people saying, "I'm too stressed out", "I'm not feeling good", I've got lots of pressure in my office", "I'm so nervous" etc. When people are stressed they feel depressed and nothing around them seems to be good. They don't like talking to someone or blame God why all this happens with them only. But if stress is handled properly it can be beneficial for us. High level of stress can be dangerous but healthy levels of stress can pump up both body and mind.

When I was in school my classmate had shared story of his grandmother. His grandmother was very weak and flimsy; she was not able to walk so all the time she used to sleep on her bed. She gets everything on her bed, her tea, breakfast, lunch, fresh n up, bathing everything at one place. But what was astonishing to him and his family was when once earthquake came, everybody was running outside their houses to save their life and his grandmother suddenly stood up on his legs and started running towards the gate. And she actually came out from house barefoot on her own. Strange right!!! But this is the fact. Earthquake here was a stressful situation for grandmother but her body responds to it positively by giving all energy to get up and run. This is body's hormonal reaction to stress or uncertainty which helped her to evolve to survive.

In short term it can energize us, revive up our system to handle what we have to do. Whenever we face stressful situations, our body responses and stimulates adrenalin which rushes in our blood, our senses become sharp and alert, mind starts working faster and its efficiency improves and heart starts beating faster. If all this is taken into a positive direction to take a step to save ourselves, stress is beneficial and if we set back and say "I can't do anything over it, it's my destiny" then the game is over. Stress has taken control of your mind. The ability to handle stress varies from person to person and one cannot measure up and allow only so much of stress while avoiding the more intense one. That is not in your hands. However, it is in your hands to train yourself for handling stress better. This would make all the difference. For example, if you find that you are responding excessively stressful to mundane matters and not proving to be effective, it is possible to adjust the way you respond. The key to reap the benefits of stress is finding just the right balance between too much and too little.

> *"Stress is not what happens to us. It's our response TO what happens. And RESPONSE is something we can choose."*
> —*Maureen Killran*

If we look into the lives of Thomas Edison, Steve Jobs, Mahatma Gandhi, Bhagat Singh, Nelson Mandela, Michael Jordan etc we'll find that these people have also faced many stressful situations coming into their lives but what makes them different from all is their RESPONSE, They responded to stress in a positive manner which had evolved their immune system to fight back and lead the path. Stress actually triggers "fight or flight" hormones that will improve the performance and protect our health. Stress makes you alert, boosts your immune system and keeps your brain cells active. Identify those things that you can control, accept the things that are out of your hands and no matter what, don't panic. Work on the things you can control and let go of the things that are out of your control.

Stress is like a muscle, exercise it too little and it cannot hold up to the strain when things get heavy. If a person is not stressed ever, then when something happens to cause stress, their body looses control and they fall apart. This could explain why some people shine in stressful situations while others collapse in panic and confusion. If our minds are totally calm and relaxed, they don't need a reason to see things differently, we're likely to feel an increase in stress when we hit on a new path, because change is typically associated with new stress.

Always remember stress illuminates your values. So listen to what your stress is trying to tell you. But it's also hard to hear your intuition when you're stressed, give yourself a break—take along walk, get a good night sleep, call a friend or just eat what you like. A person in sales job is not doing good but when the same person is criticized by his boss of not having good sales and getting feel ashamed in front of all his colleagues, stress is busted in his mind and he takes it as a challenge and in the very next month his sales were highest among all. This is very common scenario I've seen when I worked at bank. Without enough stress you're unlikely to give your full effort and you may also be prone to making mistakes. If you're too comfortable that can be a sign that you aren't pushing yourself outside your comfort zone and taking the risks necessary to advance yourself.

So, what's your toll on stress now???

3rd Meeting

It was Sunday evening. Nysha maam was sitting in Café Coffee Day waiting for Rajveer to come. And as usual today also he was late. Nysha maam was sitting at sofa set placed at the corner of CCD. Two walls of CCD were made of glass through which one can see the outer world of CCD. There was a circle facing one side of it and lots of cars, bikes and scooty's were passing by. Nysha maam was waiting and as soon as she slid down her face to see the time on her wrist watch; Rajveer had arrived.

This time Rajveer said nothing but hold his both ears with his hands to say sorry and she just smiled back. For around 30 seconds both were looking outside the glass wall and soon the silence broke.

"You like this place?" she asked.

"Yes, I love it," Rajveer answered cheerfully.

"What's so special about this place?" she asked politely.

"I and my friends use to hang out over here for long hours, we use to chat, talk over our girlfriends, latest movies, another couple sitting beside us, new car in the market and many more and while doing so I've spend most of my college days over here," Rajveer replied with excitement.

"When was the last time you came here?" Nysha maam asked.

"Hmmmmmm (thinking to get an answer of the question) may be 2 years back, I don't remember exactly," Rajveer said.

"2 years back?? Such a long time? You like this place so much, you hang out with your friends; then what is it that have bring you to a halt to visit this place again?" Nysha maam asked showing a sign of wrinkle on her forehead.

"Many things have happened with me in my past and now they had detained my brain and now I can't concentrate on anything," Rajveer said.

"I know what have happened to you. You're doing a job which you hate, your girlfriend got married, your parents fight like dogs and now you have no more friends; isn't it?" Nysha maam said in just one throw and then took a breath.

"Yes."

"So what is the big deal in this? Life hasn't stopped, you haven't stopped living, you haven't stopped eating or bathing; so why are you so much depressed? Life is not over yet. It still has so many colors to show," she said.

"It's very easy to say but it's very hard to live a life with so much unwanted happenings," Rajveer said in agitation.

"Ok! If this is the condition then it's good for you," Nysha maam shrugged.

"What is so good about it?"

"You don't remember our last session?"

"Yes. Last time we talked about stress," Then reminding the last session in his mind he continued, "Oh yes!! So you mean this is the stressful situation and I'll get something good from it."

"Yesss"

"Then tell me what is it?" Rajveer asked eagerly.

"First tell me do you share your feelings with someone?" Nysha maam asked and meanwhile called the waiter and ordered for 2 cups of coffee and 2 sandwiches.

"Earlier I use to share with one of my friend Neeraj but for the last few months I've not contacted him and now I'm all alone," Rajveer said.

"Rajveer. Have you heard this phrase? Remedy for any disease is at home. Now you have the disease of the so called depression and as the phrase goes your remedy also starts at your home," Nysha maam clarified.

"There is no one at my home except me."

"You have your parents, you live with them, right??" Nysha maam said.

"Yes I live with them but for me they don't exist," Rajveer replied.

Meanwhile their order was placed on the table.

"Look Rajveer, this is your perspective. Have you ever empathizes on their situation? Have you seen the life through their eyes? Have you ever put yourself into their shoes? Have you ever talked to any one of them about their problem?" Nysha maam asked.

"No, I never attempted to do that," Rajveer replied.

"Then do it. First talk to them, get to know about their problems, their feelings and then share yours," Nysha maam suggested.

"I'm not sure but if you say so I'll give it a try since I've never shared with them before," Rajveer said while taking his cup of coffee.

"Well, you haven't shared with me before either. You hardly know about me except that I'm a psychological consultant but today you're sitting here and sharing with me. And if you can share with me, I'm sure you can do with your parents too," she further says, "Nothing is impossible. You just have to take the first steps and you can see the ladder clearly. Take the charge and talk with them. First understand them and then try to get understood," Nysha maam said sensitively.

She further stated, "Some people are close to their parents while some are very close to their friends. Firstly, go and talk with your parents and if you don't get a solution; contact your friend Neeraj and share with him about your life and your feelings. I'm sure you'll get some help."

"But I don't have Neeraj's contact and it's been months we've talked to each other," Rajveer said while shrugging his shoulder and ate a bite of sandwich.

"C'mon Rajveer!! Do I really need to tell you how to contact your best friend? Call your other friends and get his number, go at his home, login to face book and search about him. There are end numbers of ways to find a person you're very close with," Nysha maam said while taking a back on the sofa with her cup of coffee.

"Ok Ok Nysha Ji; I'll do it," Rajveer said in a convincing tone.

"Now that's better," Nysha maam said.

I always use to share my worries with my mother and as Nysha maam says, I really get the solution within minutes. I must say my mother is genius. She is my Lifeline.

"Lifeline" This is about what Nysha maam further said.

"Whenever you're in trouble, use your lifeline, talk to your parents, call your friend, go to your neighbour hood for some help, consult an expert and if no one else is there, still you are never alone; GOD is always there for you," Nysha maam said taking her last sip of coffee.

And these lifelines took over 1 more hour further with 2 more cups of coffee.

CHAPTER 3

Lifelines

Imagine a scene of an ICU room in a hospital where a patient who'd recently got a heart attack is lying on the bed. Around him are lying all different types of machines which are trying to keep him alive which include oxygen mask, incubator, blood supply, ECG machine and many more. Here the patient is fighting for his life and all these machines and equipments are acting as lifelines to save his life and support him to get back to its normal state. In the same way, life is full of ups and downs, at times we are happy and at times we are depressed. In our daily routine life we face so many situations like passing a board exam, having a good relationship, promotion in salary, getting married, break ups, sex scandals, death of a dear one etc which gives us different feeling at that moment and either we get excited or get emotionally imbalanced. To come back to our normal state during emotional imbalance we need certain machines called lifelines to take ourselves in first gear and move on in life rather than sticking at one point or going to reverse gear.

You all must know about the famous game Kaun Banega Crorepati (KBC). Here in people come across the country and participate to reach the final stage and win the lottery, but people need certain help to reach at the final stage. So the host of the show Mr. Amitabh Bacchhan provides the help of lifelines to the participants to be used at different stage of the game to achieve the final destination. Similarly, our life is also a game, we are just a character send to the earth by GOD to play the game of life and understand the rules and regulations of life and to reach the final goal, the ultimate destination. The final goal can be different for different people, it might be to become a doctor or engineer and serve the people, to become a politician, to become a good daughter, wife and mother all over your life, to earn lots and lots of money, to become an entrepreneur or to win in Olympics. For a journey, destination may vary and so does the route but the basic necessity will be the same i.e. air, food and water to complete the journey. And these basic necessities act as lifelines to complete our path, to fight against all odds and to win over the journey of life.

So similar to KBC, here I bring to you the lifelines you can use at any stage of your life. Use them whenever or wherever you feel its need and I'm sure many of you had already used it at certain stage of life and many of you will be using it in future to live life a better way.

1. Parent's Pole

We become a part of this Universe because our parents gave us birth. We are healthy, active and able to speak because our parents take care of us. We are able to read and write because our parents hold our hands to get in the schools. We are able to pursue higher education because they sacrifice their needs and pay our huge fees. We are able to sit in McDonalds or Barista and eat our favorite pizza and drink coffee because our parents give us pocket money. Parents do everything for us. They don't bother about themselves but they get worried about us. They know every single habit of ours, what we like, what we don't like, what is the thing which cause allergy to us, what's going on in our mind, they know everything because its they who have nurtured us. We are like tiny seeds to them to whom they had given proper food, shelter, appropriate environment to make us grow healthy, fit and fine, to make us physically, mentally and emotionally strong.

STORY

A young man was getting ready to graduate college. For many months he had admired a beautiful sports car in a dealer's showroom, and knowing his father could well afford it, he told him that was all he wanted. As Graduation Day approached, the young man awaited signs that his father had purchased the car. Finally, on the morning of his graduation his father called him into his private study. His father told him how proud he was to have such a fine son, and told him how much he loved him. He handed his son a beautiful wrapped gift box.

Curious, but somewhat disappointed the young man opened the box and found a lovely, leather-bound Bible. Angrily, he raised his voice at his father and said, "With all your money you give me a Bible?" and stormed out of the house, leaving the holy book.

Many years passed and the young man was very successful in business. He had a beautiful home and wonderful family, but realized his father was very old, and thought perhaps he should go to him. He had not seen him since that graduation day. Before he could make arrangements, he received a telegram telling him his father had passed away, and willed all of his possessions to his son. He needed to come home immediately and take care of the things. When he arrived at his father's house, sudden sadness and regret filled his heart.

He began to search his father's important papers and saw the still new Bible, just as he had left it years ago. With tears, he opened the Bible and began to turn the pages. As he read those words, a car key dropped from an envelope taped behind the Bible. It had a tag with the dealer's name, the same dealer who had the sports car he had desired. On the tag was the date of his graduation, and the words . . . PAID IN FULL?

So our first lifeline is our Parents. Some of you might be close to your father or your mother but your parents are only close to you. You are their world and they see nothing beyond you. At any point of your life, whenever you face any problem or you're in a dilemma, consult it to your parents, tell them what you feel and what you want because they'll understand you better and can do anything for you. They'll give you right advice, avoids you to go on a wrong path and will show faith in you and direct you to the right path.

I remember in my childhood days, when I was feeling so hungry and I badly needed something to eat, my mother came in my room, saw my dull face and asked what happened. I said, "I am feeling very hungry." My mother said, "Wait, I'll come back in few minutes." She went to the kitchen and after few minutes she was with a dish in her hand. And to my surprise it was my favorite dish, Maggi. I didn't know how she knew that I was in need of maggi at that very moment. I finished the whole dish and now my tummy was full. In many cases like this, we don't know what we want but our parents do know us. When we grow up and come back from office and we feel hungry, it's very hard to cook something for ourselves. But we feel very great when we come back from office and we are served with our favorite dinner on dining table and fill our appetite. And that dinner on the table is of course because of our parents. At any point of time, our spouse may leave us because of certain habits or uncertainty or our children may leave us because they feel we are old now but our parents will never leave us.

> *"My heroes are and were my parents. I can't see having anyone else as my heroes."*
> *—Michael Jordan*

Our parents raise us all over again, build self esteem within us, make ourselves connected to rest of the world, fly kites with us, seriously play with us, make is ensure that we can reach the stars and always hug us whenever we need, So always love them, share with them, tell them how much you love your parents and trust me they are the first person to be in queue when you're asked, "Who supports you?" They are first gear of our life who gives us kick start to move on. And as Billy Graham has said, "A child who is allowed to be disrespectful to his parents will not have true respect for anyone," make your parents your models, you need not to search for a big personality or a professional athlete whom you would like to be, and rather you first need to be like your parents.

STORY: An Apple Tree

A long time ago, there was a huge apple tree. A little boy loved to come and play around it everyday. He climbed to the treetop, ate the apples, and took a nap under the shadow. He loved the tree and the tree loved to play with him. Time went by, the little boy had grown up and he no longer played around the tree every day. One day, the boy came back to the tree and he looked sad. "Come and play with me", the tree asked the boy. "I am no longer a kid, I do not play around trees any more" the boy replied. "I want toys. I need money to buy them." "Sorry, but I do not have money; but you can pick all my apples and sell them. So, you will have money." The boy was so excited. He grabbed all the apples on the tree and left happily. The boy never came back after he picked the apples. The tree was sad.

One day, the boy who now turned into a man returned and the tree was excited. "Come and play with me" the tree said. "I do not have time to play. I have to work for my family. We need a house for shelter. Can you help me?" "Sorry, but I do not have any house. But you can chop off my branches to build your house". So the man cut all the branches of the tree and left happily. The tree was glad to see him happy but the man never came back since then. The tree was again lonely and sad.

One hot summer day, the man returned and the tree was delighted. "Come and play with me!" the tree said. "I am getting old. I want to go sailing to relax myself. Can you give me a boat?" said the man. "Use my trunk to build your boat. You can sail far away and be happy." So the man cut the tree trunk to make a boat. He went sailing and never showed up for a long time.

Finally, the man returned after many years. "Sorry my boy, But I do not have anything for you anymore. No more apples for you", the tree said. "No problem, I do not have any teeth to bite" the man replied. "No more trunk for you to climb on". "I am too old for that now" the man said. "I really cannot give you anything, the only thing left is my dying roots," the tree said with tears. "I do not need much now, just a place to rest. I am tired after all these years," the man replied. "Good! Old tree roots are the best place to lean on and rest, come sit down with me and rest." The man sat down and the tree was glad and smiled with tears.

⊷ ❈ ⊶

This is a story of everyone. The apple tree is like our parents. When we were young, we loved to play with our Mum and Dad. When we grow up, we leave them; only come to them when we need something or when we are in trouble.

No matter what, parents will always be there and give everything they could just to make you happy. You may think the boy is cruel to the apple tree, but that is how all of us treat our parents. We take them for granted; we don't appreciate all they do for us, until it's too late.

- Tell your parents every morning that you love them.
- Remember that they brought you in this world.
- Respect them and cherish all good moments with them.
- Share your feelings with them.
- Give your time to your parents, talk to them.
- Forgive your parents if they had made any mistake. After all they are human beings.
- Go out with your parents and have a dinner tonight with them.
- Listen to their old stories and learn from them.
- After all your parents are everything, make them your own world.

2. Phone a Friend

> *"A single rose can be my garden . . . .*
> *a single friend, my world."*
> **—Leo Buscaglia**

When we were in school, we made friends. We went to high school, again we made some friends. We went to college and it again added many names to the friend's list. We work in office or do some business; we make our colleagues and our customers our friends. Some are very close to us while some are by the way friends. At every stage of our life, we needed help of our friends. Let it be to borrow a pen, go in a disco, propose to your girlfriend, arrangement of money to start a business, for finding perfect match for your child, helping to choose your best insurance plan and to make you feel how important you are to them. After getting into the school we stay more connected to our friends, we start sharing our thoughts, likes and dislikes with them, we spent most of the time with them and get to know about each other. Eventually, they become our part and we can't imagine our life without friends. It's like eating food with no spices. Friends are the most important ingredient in the recipe of our life.

As Laurence J. Peter says, "You can always tell a real friend, when you've made a fool of yourself, he doesn't feel you've done a permanent job." Your true friends are the one who accepts you the way you are, believes in you, calls you just to say Hiii, forgives your mistakes, helps you all the time whenever you're in need, loves you for what you are, raises your spirit, tells you what should be done at the very moment, understands you, value you, walk besides you, explains you when you don't understand, yells at you when you don't listen, gives everything to you without asking, knows you better than you and overall makes a difference in your life.

> *"One loyal friend is worth ten thousand relatives."*
>
> *—Euripides*

Friends are a very rare jewel, indeed. They make you smile and encourage you to succeed. They lend an ear, they share a word of praise, and they always want to open their hearts to us. To live life a better way is a challenging task since we encounter many odds and outs in our way and we struggle for many things to get what we want. At times we are happy and at times we are depressed. We have our family to help us and support us but there are many issues which you can't share with your parents like when you fall in love with a girl/boy, your best friend would be the first person to know this and will surely help you in any manner.

We can't share some topics with our parents but we can share any topic with our friends. Friends may not save, but they never let you go too deep. Your friend is the first person to clear your doubts in college, your friend is the first person to help you go to your first date, your friend is the first person to cheer you when you make a record, your friend is the first person to ask you for a treat when you failed, your friend is the first person to make you laugh by his silly jokes when you're crying.

So whenever you face any problem or stuck in any trouble, and when you don't know what to do now, just call your one of the best friend and tell him about your situation and get easy because now your trouble is not yours its your friend's trouble now and he'll definitely get you out of it. As it is said, a good friend is cheaper than therapy. Don't go in hospitals and pay your bills only because you're depressed, just call your friend. A friend can cheer us when we are depressed or sorrowful. A friend can motivate us when we give up. So whenever from now you feel that your life is being so unpleasant to you, just go around with your friend to have a good time, to laugh, to act silly and enrich your lives.

> *"What is a friend? A single soul dwelling in two bodies."*
>
> —*Aristotle*

Your true friend is simply your self in disguise. By uncovering that disguise you see before your eyes the world you created and the being you've become. So in how many ways your friends have made you feel loved, accepted, respected and care for? Probably, too many to list and the list grows daily. Think of your true friends and be grateful for the gifts they bring into your life. Allow your hearts to connect and bring comfort to each other. Give them your love in return, for each friend you have is an unearned gift that should be accepted with grace and thankfulness as each friend represents a world within us. And always use Triple Filter Test what Socrates use while listening about friends.

STORY: *Filter Test*

In ancient Greece, Socrates was reputed to hold knowledge in high esteem. One day one fellow met the great philosopher and said, "Do you know what I just heard about your friend?" "Hold on a minute," Socrates replied. "Before telling me anything I'd like you to pass a little test. It's called the Triple Filter Test. "Triple filter?" "That's right," Socrates continued. "Before you talk to me about my friend, it might be a good idea to take a moment and filter what you're going to say. That's why I call it the triple filter test. The first filter is Truth. Have you made absolutely sure that what you are about to tell me is true?" "No," the man said, "actually I just heard about it and . . ." "All right," said Socrates. "So you don't know if it's true or not. Now let's try the second filter, the filter of Goodness. Is what you are about to tell me about my friend something good?" "No on the contrary." "So," Socrates continued, "you want to tell me something bad about him, but you're not certain it's true. You may still pass the test though, because there's one filter left: the filter of Usefulness. Is what you want to tell me about my friend going to be useful to me?" "No not really." "Well," concluded Socrates, "if what you want to tell me is neither true nor good nor even useful, why tell it to me at all?"

Lesson:

Well we can always participate in loose talks to curb our boredom. But when it comes to you friends it's not worth it. Always avoid talking behind the back about your near and dear friends.

3. Expert (Teacher) Advice

> *"Every truth has four corners: as a teacher*
> *I give you one corner, and it's for you to*
> *find the other three."*
>
> *—Confucius*

In KBC when participants got stuck in answering the question, they use lifelines and this time it was expert advice. In expert advice, they refer a personality who had got expertise in some or the other field and the participant can take the help of expert to answer the question and move on. Similarly, in our life also we got stuck at some moment of time and we need to refer experts in our life. And to experts I mean our teachers, our Guru who had given us basic fundamental education in schools and art of living and wisdom when we did graduation.

At some point of time, we also get personal with our teachers, we get close to them and they get to know us better. To them, we are like seeds and they exactly know what kind of seed we are, so accordingly they nurture us with appropriate soil, water, food and environment. They very well know how to treat us, what method cold be used to make us understand certain thing, how to motivate us etc. The difference between the ordinary and the extra ordinary is the little extra. I'm not talking about the ordinary teacher you met in your life and just taught you how to read and write because it was his duty and responsibility but I'm talking about the extra ordinary teacher who knows you what you are, for what you're passionate, what is that thing that brings spark in you. Our teachers are very experienced and had already gone through the stage over which we are walking now.

You had already taken help of your parents, your friends and its turn of your teacher. Because your friends are of same age as you are, they also might be experiencing the same thing what you are facing or feeling the same way what you're feeling now, although you can share with them but the solution can be given by your expert, your teacher.

> *"The mediocre teacher tells. The good teacher explains. The superior teacher demonstrates. The greater teacher inspires."*
> —*William Arthur Ward*

Always remember your teacher is like a candle who consumes itself to light the way for you. There is a very strong relationship between teacher and student and if we adopt ourselves to carry it well we will find that we've got another beautiful person in our life who understands us very well. A great teacher will always be there to support you, will always be accessible whenever you want to meet and talk. And I believe teaching and understanding your students is the greatest art of all since the medium is human mind and spirit.

As Aristotle had rightly said, "Those who educate children well are more to be honored then parents, for those only gave life, those art of living well." As it is the art of teacher to awaken the very self within ourselves, to know our creativity and awaken the sense of joy and happiness in our every moment. So the next time feel like you need help of someone, go to one of your teacher and share with them your problem and be sure you'll be the bird after that and your wings will open wide and fly in the sky of freedom and tension free life.

> *"A single conversation across the table with a wise man is worth a month's study of books."*
>
> *—Chinese Proverb*

4. Lifeline of All

By now, we have used all the lifelines and had taken help from our parents, friends, and relatives and even from our best teachers who are expert in some or the other field. Yet there are many people who say that they are still in trouble, it seems as if the whole burden is on their shoulders. They feel very depressed, discouraged and lonely. They say they'd already used these lifelines but couldn't be able to reach the jackpot and enjoy the life at the fullest. My advice to them is, "This is not the end, and this is just the beginning." Don't think that all your lifelines were worth using since you got no solution. No, don't even think that. Your lifelines must have helped you in some or the other way. Still I got some more powerful tonic for you and this is lifeline of all lifelines.

All the majestic power lies in His hand. We are here because of Him; the world is created because of Him; we find joyful and happiest moments because of Him; we get what we want because of Him. By now you must have understood whom I am talking about. Yes it's the eternal power, the Almighty, the GOD.

When you feel that you're in a trap and you find no other way to get rid of it, just close your eyes and remember GOD and say him, "I Love You, I know if I am here its because you wanted me to be exactly here in this situation. Thank you very much for always being with me." You might be thinking that while we are in trouble how we can say such words to GOD because we usually blame him. This is what we have to remember that whatever is happening with us is because He wants us to be like that. The real fact is our plans for ourselves are meager in front of God's plans for us. Whatever He does, there is something very good behind that purpose which we can't foresee or imagine. He is the one who created us and He knows better what is good for us and what is bad, what should be done and what not. Just believe in GOD and his plans for you. When you find no way ahead remember GOD is there to help you.

GOD is like aspirin, he works miracles. GOD is like ford, he's got a better idea. GOD is like coke, he's a real thing. GOD is like hallmark cards, he cares enough to send his very best. GOD is like tide, he gets the stain out that others leave behind. GOD is like General Electric, he brings good thing to life. GOD is like post office, neither rain nor pain nor sleet nor ice will keep Him from His appointed destination. GOD is the one who understands our prayer even when we don't find the words to say Him.

⊷❈⊷

STORY: God gives everything for our own good

A king had a wise, pious and faithful minister. The king trusted him but disliked his frequent statement, "God gives everything for our own good."

Once they went together for hunting. While making a way through the forest by cutting the bushes with his sword, the king cut off the tip of his middle finger. They treated the wound using medicinal herbs and bandaged the wound to stop bleeding. As they finished the treatment, the minister made his usual remark, "God gives everything for our own good." The king was furious. "You are really cruel", he said, "I am in great pain and you say it is for good. You will say the same thing when I lose my head!" Filled with rage, he flung the minister into a dirty pit and raced off alone.

In the dense forest, the king was caught by a group of savages. They tied him up and carried him to their chieftain. They were celebrating a religious festival. They wanted to offer the king as a human sacrifice before their deity. As the rituals were progressing, the chief priest examined the 'offering' in detail and found out that the tip of his middle finger was missing. He declared that only perfect bodies without any defect would be acceptable as sacrifice before the deity.

Hence the king was released. The king realized that the minister's statement was correct. So he returned to the pit and rescued the minister. The king narrated the events and apologized for his action. The minister repeated, "God gives everything for our own good."

The king asked for an explanation for this statement. The minister said, "If you had not put me in the pit, I would have been with you when the savages attacked and they would have sacrificed me instead of you!" The king now confessed with conviction, "You are correct. God gives everything for our own good."

God has a definite plan for every man, a plan to bring prosperity and not disaster.

Don't Limit God

As we have read above story we got to know that GOD gives everything for our own good. GOD has his own plans for us. So we should never under estimate GOD and His actions for us. Whatever He does at whatever time in whatsoever manner is the best thing done with us at His best time. GOD always says to us, "You are limiting me what I can do with you because of your small thinking." We always ask to GOD for some or the other thing like a good job, a good partner, a well furnished home or a promotion. But what we should really do is thank Him for whatever He had given us and enjoy in every single moment and ask him for a better health, a working mind, respect for others, love for others, patience, peace, strength etc. Don't limit yourselves only to materialistic things and don't ask for anything because may be you ask him for a thousand rupees but you're worth of one lakh rupees. But since you've asked for only thousand, you'll get only thousand. So never limit your thinking and never limit God's power. As C.S. Lewis says, "Though our feelings come and go, God's love for us does not."

So now it's the turn to use this lifeline at every stage of life whenever we are in despair, trust GOD that he is there and standing beside us to help us and show us the right direction. As Eleanor Powell says, "What we are is God's gift to us, what we become is our gift to God."

STORY: GOD Is Listening

A woman was at work when she received a phone call that her small daughter is very sick with a fever. She left her work and stopped by the pharmacy to get some medication. She got back to the car and found that she had locked her keys in the car. She didn't know what to do, so she called home and told the babysitter what had happened.

The baby sitter told her that the fever was getting worse. She said, "You might find a coat hanger and use that to open the door."

The woman looked around and found an old rusty coat hanger that had been left on the ground, possibly by someone else who had sometime had locked their keys in their car. She looked at the hanger and said, "I don't know how to use this."

She prayed to God and asked Him to send her help.

Within five minutes a beat up old motorcycle pulled up, with a dirty, greasy, bearded man who was wearing an old biker skull rag on his head.

The woman thought, "This is what you sent to help me?" But, she was desperate, so she kept quite.

The man got off of his cycle and asked if he could help. She said, "Yes, my daughter is very sick . . . I stopped to get her some medication and I locked my keys in my car. I must get home to her. Please, can you use this hanger to unlock my car?"

He said, "Sure." He walked over to the car, and within a minute the car was opened.

She thanked the man and through her tears she said, "Thank you so much! You are a very nice man."

The man replied, "Lady, I am not a nice man. I just got out of prison today. I was in prison for car theft and have only been out for about an hour."

The woman thanked the man again and with sobbing tears cried out loud, "Oh, Thank you GOD! You even sent me a professional!"

Moral: Always have trust in GOD, pray to Him and be patient. He would help us from sources which we never could have imagined.

4th Meeting

"May I come in Nysha Ji?" Rajveer opened the gate and greeted excitedly.

Nysha maam was working on her laptop and suddenly the door was opened in one shot and she looked above and then she turned her face towards right to watch the time. It was 4'o clock, exactly on time. I was shocked how come Rajveer came on time today.

"Please come in Rajveer. You're right on time, impressive!" Nysha maam said with her eyebrows lifted above.

Today Rajveer was looking stunning. He was wearing dark blue denim jeans, grey coloured T-shirt marked UCB on it and sporty shoes.

Rajveer stepped in a heroic way, took the seat opposite to Nysha maam and said, "Thank you Ji, I thought let's be punctual this time so here I am."

This boy is not too bad; I thought in my mind. He was educated, rich, good looking, decent and smart. The only thing was that he was disheartened which had stolen the spark from his face and made him look like an ordinary one. He was strong from outside but was broken from within.

"So how are you feeling today?" Nysha maam asked.

I don't understand why she asks such questions? Was he ill or something or coming back from hospital or it was just asked to begin the conversation?

"I'm all good," Rajveer replied.

"So have you talked to your parents?" Nysha maam inquired.

"No; not yet, I'm not getting the feeling to talk to them. I thought about it but left that thought within few minutes only." Rajveer said half-heartedly.

"That's OK. Initially you'll find it tough but ultimately you can do it. They are not ghosts or dinosaurs or person from other planet. They are your parents and will always be. Take your time but this time extend your thinking time." Nysha maam said politely.

"Ok I will," Rajveer nodded.

"Alright Rajveer. I wanted to know something more about you. You had already shared your problems with me and now you yourself will share the solution to me," Nysha maam said simply.

Although she said it simply; but it was not simple for me. This was taking a toll in my mind and I was thinking if

Rajveer had the solution then how come he doesn't know it and if he knows it then why he is here. Anyways this is my wandering mind and that is Nysha maam's; she must have something in her mind.

"I will tell you the solution? If I would have known it, then why I am here?" he said and was looking astounded.

"The solution is with you and you'll know it eventually as we continue talking," again she said it simply while grinning.

"You know Nysha Ji, sometimes your mysterious talk goes above my head; I don't get it instantly. Anyways, I trust you so let it be the way you want it," Rajveer conceded.

"Well that's good" she said in appreciation and further continued, "now tell me about your past, your school and college days, your job, friends, girlfriend. I mean share with me some of your happy moments, achievements and certain failures if you have any."

"You wanted to know more about me?" Rajveer asked.

"Yes, I wanted to know you thoroughly," she replied.

"Ok. So let me begin with aaaa . . . . . (Taking a pause to rethink about from where to start) and after a nano break he begins, "I was very bad in my studies. In every standard I use to fail in one or two subjects compulsorily and my teachers had to push me through grace to proceed to next class. That was OK with me as I had the least interest in studies but it was not the same with my dad. He used to scold me and beat me with stick and start comparing me with other boys who got good marks. Till 8th standard it continued like this only but when I came in 9th; I was failed. My dad was in shock because other students (sons of their colleagues) were good and he felt insulted in front of them when I failed and then a full day seminar was held between me and my dad. And my mother was listen me screaming, noise of sticks and harsh words from my dad like you are a shame, you can't do anything; you had lost my money spent on you and all that stuff. And that day I decided to prove him wrong and take out his misconceptions about me. From that day I studied with keen interest and left all games and ultimately I scored 82% in 10th standard," Rajveer said.

"That sounds great. I appreciate you on that," Nysha maam said indulgently.

"Thank You," Rajveer said.

Rajveer's eyes twinkled with a sense of victory as if he'd won some world cup or something like that.

He further stated, "Later I did MBA course wherein I was the head of entrepreneurship club and I was responsible for its event to be organized every 2 months. I had a team and a plan too. This time I proposed for the business plan game. Every participant was given Rs.1000 and they have to do certain business for 15 days and try to increase the profits as much as possible to beat their competitors. My mentor approved it and that month was a blast. Our dean also liked it so much. Some was selling chats and bhelpuri's while some was spreading fragrance by selling roses; some sold imitated jewellery while some go for stationery. All went good and all of them earned profits. Ultimately I was awarded a cash prize by our dean for this phenomenal plan."

"Well, this is really innovative; I really liked it," she expressed.

"Rajveer, you remember during our first meting you said you're an Empty Idiot Box; I guess you're not. You're quite intelligent, creative, smart and even bold; it's just that you need a proper guidance," Nysha maam believed.

"Do you really think I'm worth it?" Rajveer asked in deep husky voice.

"Yes, you're worth it. You are a diamond. You just need proper polishing, handling and care," Nysha maam declared.

"Ok now tell me one thing you love to do," Nysha maam asked.

"I love my body very much. I love to do exercising and gyming. In fact I use to go to gym at least 5 days a week. You can say it was a ritual for me to practice it daily. But for now I've left everything," Rajveer replied.

"If you really liked it so much then why did you discontinue?" Nysha maam asked surprisingly.

"I don't know. I don't feel like doing anything now," Rajveer said in a low voice.

Nysha maam nodded and was trying to understand his phase through which he was going through.

"Ok now tell me something about your girlfriend," Nysha maam asked and this time she stood up from her chair and moved towards the large glass window and signaled Rajveer to move there.

"I don't want to talk anything about her," Rajveer protested still sitting on his chair.

"Relax Rajveer, I'm not forcing you. If you're not comfortable at it; leave it," Nysha maam said.

Rajveer nodded and said nothing.

I figured out Rajveer was conscious this time. I guess his girlfriend is the main reason for his depression. I know the boys, initially they are playboys but once they'd fallen in love with someone; they get so possessive about the girl and if the girl leaves the boy; he is for sure going to be in the lake of gloominess.

"Alright Rajveer, now that you've shared your life with me; I'll share the solutions with you. These solutions are actually within you but you're not aware of it but don't worry I'll do it for you," Nysha maam said while standing beside the glass window and signaled Rajveer to come and sit on the sofa.

Rajveer stood up from the chair and moved towards the sofa.

"Rajveer have you ever seen an ECG machine showing heart beat of a person? The machine displays the linings going up and down in an uncertain manner which means that the person is living and the moment that line goes straight; the person is dead. Similarly in our life too we have many ups and downs, we go through certain failures and also taste success which makes us strong through our course of life," Nysha maam explained while using her hands to show up and down of the curves of an ECG machine.

Rajveer sat on the sofa and was blinking his eyes and looked towards Nysha maam in sense of getting understand what she was saying.

"You are still too young Rajveer, you have to face many of the situations in future which make you strong internally and externally only if you wish to learn from everything that comes along your way," she further clarified.

Rajveer was listening quietly and carefully as if a sincere student was sitting in the first row of class and paying attention to what his teacher was elucidating.

"In your life Rajveer, you'd tasted the failure when you failed in 9th standard which stroke you to get better results in 10th and you scored very well unexpectedly. What if you haven't failed; you'll not be able to light your inner fire and it goes on as it used to be earlier to fail in one or two subjects," Nysha maam explained while taking a seat on nearby sofa.

"This failure was your first stepping stone which kindle the fire of dedication, determination and commitment to prove to your father that Yes, you can do it," she said simply.

"Isn't it?" Nysha maam asked.

"Yes, you are right. I haven't given it a thought the way you did it," Rajveer conceded.

I never failed in exams in fact I was the topper of my class and it still makes me feel proud about it and my other classmates use to bring chocolates and offer me ice-cream so that I can share my notes with them.

"Always remember one thing, never get afraid or feel awful about your failure; rather feel happy about it that you're progressing towards success," Nysha maam suggested.

"Point to be noted Nysha Ji," Rajveer responded.

"Secondly, I must say you're a very intelligent and creative person. You are the master of your life. So if you don't like your barking boss; just leave him. Listen to your heart, get to know your inner instincts and follow them. Do the work you love and you don't have to work for any single day rather you'll enjoy doing it," Nysha maam clarified.

"But what should I do?" Rajveer asked.

"I'll give you a way through it. List 10 things you love to do. Read them again and again and get to know what is it that gives you happiness or fills you with joy; make a plan over it and start doing it and you can also make a business out of it," Nysha maam said.

"Business? Like what??" Rajveer asked and looked perplexed.

"Like, if you like cooking, be a chef; if you like partying and meeting friends, open a restaurant; if you like exercising, be a trainer and open your gym; if you like writing, be a author or if you like traveling, be a guide. Now you've to make a list what you actually like and then find out the ways to convert your likings into business or a venture," Nysha maam said.

"I like exercising, in fact I love doing it. Can I make a business out of it?" Rajveer said instantly.

"Yes, you can" she replied.

"But how?"

"That I will leave up to you; let your brain squeeze this time," Nysha maam giggled.

Rajveer smiled too.

"Last but very important, love yourself and believe in yourself. Never let others make you feel about yourself.

You know yourself better than others and always say "I am the best." Don't let your past overtake your mind. I know you are deeply affected by the act of your girlfriend but that's not the end of life. I know it's tough but not unavoidable. Be open to others and allow more life to enter and add flavours to your life," Nysha maam said simply.

Wow, so simple yet so powerful. She is perfectly right; life is not that too bad. It's just our perspective to how we see to it. What if one person implements all these principles into one's life; life will be so easy going.

"Now I got you Nysha Ji. My answers and my solutions were within my problems. It was your outlook that has identified it," Rajveer said.

Nysha maam nodded and feeling good that Rajveer understood the point what she was trying to clarify.

Their session was helpful for me too. I was also trying to get insights within me and was pondering on what I should do now; I started putting light on my life too. According to Nysha maam, failure is the first step toward success. If you haven't tasted failure yet, be sure you're going on the right path; and if you're tasting failure again and again, be sure that you're moving towards success at full pace.

CHAPTER 4

Embrace Failure

"Failure doesn't mean you're failure, it just means you have not succeeded yet."
— *Robert Schuller*

It is said that behind every successful man there is a woman. But I do not consider this. Rather, I would say behind every successful man/woman, there is series of failures. As Winston Churchill says, "Success consists of going from failure to failure without loss of enthusiasm."

Every successful man fails at sometime. Failure tells you about your weaknesses, shortcomings, lack of preparation and lack of efforts. So if you can mange to learn from failures you'll definitely reach where you started to go out. Making a mistake is not a crime, the ability to learn from it contribute to lasting success. Extract the lesson to be learnt from failure and try again with redoubled vigour. Facing failure makes oneself strong, wiser and more resolute. Every successful man has failed, not once but several times in their life, but they analyzed the thing in real perspective and tried again with more vigor and zeal and got success. Failure should not be allowed to create frustration or disappointment instead failure should be taken as a boon which gives you strength to fight back with invincible zeal.

> *"Defeat is not the worst of failure. Not to*
> *have tried is true failure."*
> *—George E. Woodberry*

Don't be afraid to fail. Don't waste energy trying to cover up failure. Learn from your failures and go to the next challenge. It's OK to fail. If you're not failing, it means you're not growing and moving on in wrong direction. Don't be discouraged by failure. It can be a positive experience. Failure; is in a sense, the highway to success.

Examples of People who got success after failure:

Thomas Edison's teacher said he was too stupid to learn anything. He was fired from his first two jobs for being "non productive". As an inventor, Edison made 1000 unsuccessful attempts at inventing the light bulb. When a reporter said, "How did it feel to fail 1000 times?" Edison replied, "I didn't failed 1000 times. The light bulb was an invention with 1000 steps."

Albert Einstein did not speak until he was 4 years old and did not read until he was 7. His teachers described him as "mentally slow, unsociable and adrift forever in foolish dreams." and now known as Father of Modern Physics.

Beethoven handled the violin awkwardly and preferred playing his own compositions instead of improving his techniques. His teacher called him "hopeless as a composer" and of course you know that he wrote 5 of his greatest symphonies while completely deaf.

Anything that comes too early to us is worth satisfying. When you want to succeed, be ready to pay the price for it. As rightly said by Burford Frank, "Failure is the tuition you pay for success." Every human being makes mistakes but rather than continuing the same mistakes again and again you need to sit and ponder upon all the lacking which caused you to fail. Analyze yourself, analyze the way you work and find out the set backs and then put in all your efforts to rectify it and then not to repeat the same mistake. For the first 22 years of your life, you are taught that mistakes are bad and embarrassing, when in fact; mistakes are simply opportunities to learn something new. The more mistakes a person makes, the more they will have learned and the greater chance they will have of succeeding on their next try. The key, however, is to learn from your mistakes and never make the same mistake twice.

> *"Character consists of what you do on the third and fourth tries."*
> —*James A. Mihanes*

> *"The man who makes no mistakes does not usually make anything."*
> —*E.J. Phelps*

Mere talking idle, day dreaming or aimless drifting will not take you to goal, but only divert your attention and dissipate your energy and strength. Hardships, obstacles, failures are the various moments in the way of success. They are not to be evaded but to face them bravely, courageously and with double dynamism.

A child can seldom learn to walk, without making sustained and sincere efforts in the process tumbling and falling down a number of times. His failures never deter him to stop standing again. The doggedness in the child's resolve lies in making any number of attempts to stand up and walk whatever be the pain or fear of fall. So let us also be like child where we don't know or don't fear of falling down, instead we have inquisitiveness inside to move forward and reach our goal.

> *"A life spent making mistakes is not only more honorable but more useful than life spend doing nothing."*
> —*George Bernard Shaw*

❧ ✄ ❧

STORY: King Bruce and Spider

Vikram was a brave king. Once, he had to fight against a large army with just a few soldiers, he was defeated. He had to run for his life.

Vikram took shelter in a forest cave. He was very depressed. His courage had left him. He was blankly gazing at the ceiling of the cave. An interesting scene captured his attention.

A small spider was trying to weave a web across the cave ceiling. As the spider crawled up, a thread of the web broke and the spider fell down. But the spider did not give up. He tried to climb again and again. Finally, the spider successfully climbed up and completed the web.

Vikram began to think, "If a small spider can face failure so bravely, why should I give up? I will try with all might till I win". This thought gave strength to the defeated king.

Vikram got out of the jungle and collected his brave soldiers. He fought against the large army. He was defeated again. But now, he would not give up his fight.

Vikram again and again fought against the large army and finally, after many attempts defeated the large army and regained his kingdom. He had learnt a lesson from the spider.

MORAL: Failure leads to success.

As said by Confucius, "Our greatest glory is not in ever failing, but in rising every time we fail." Little minds are tamed and subdued by failures, misfortunes, but great minds rise above it. You must face every adverse circumstance as its master and do not let it master you.

So failures are the pillars of success, stepping stones to success.

Human life is the story of numerous failures and a few achievements. Success naturally gives us joy and pride. Failures generally disappoint and discourage us. However, the right approach to failures is not to be disheartened by them. We should learn some lessons out of them. Each time we fail, we come to know the reasons of our failures. We become aware of our weaknesses and defeats. We also discover our hidden powers. The experience we gain each time makes our path to success smoother and easier. Thus, the failures are our best instructors, guides and teachers. They make us bold, active and vigilant. Those who fail must succeed at one day. The story of "King Bruce and the Spider" should be an eye opener.

At last I would only like to say that remember the two benefits of failure. First, if you do fail, you learn what doesn't work, and second, the failure gives you opportunity to try a new approach. And always start doing your work thinking that, "smooth roads never make food drivers, clean sky never make good pilot, problem free life never make a strong person." So don't ask life "Why Me", instead smile back at it and say "Try Me."

CHAPTER 5

Success

What is success? Success is a state of mind. To some success may be to have lots of money, to some it may mean to do world tour, to some it may mean good and healthy relationship with family and friends, while to some it may mean a hike in salary and to some success means living a good life.

For poor person success means to earn food for himself and his family at least twice a day. Once it is done, person will think that he had achieved something and got successful in feeding his family. For middle class person, success may mean to earn livelihood in order to maintain a good status in society, upbringing his children with good manners, had a back up plan for his retirement and a happy married life with his wife. For a rich person, success may mean a world tour, buying a big house or a BMW car, set up an industry etc.

In such a dynamic world where people of all castes, religion and status reside, everyone has their own definition of success. To an 18 year boy, clearing AIEEE exam is success; to an 1 year old baby, walking on his own legs is success; to a 25 year old man, getting a promotion is success; to a 75 year old man, spending his life with wife and kids is success; to a doctor who gave life to patient is success.

It all depends on what we think about it and how do we react to it. And while doing what we want to achieve, the feeling inside us is success. As it is rightly said, success is a journey and not a destination. And to me, success is getting what you want. Everybody doesn't get what one want. But if you really want something in your life, you have to give your 100% to it and then nobody can stop that thing to come towards you.

Have you ever thought why successful people are successful???

Take any name Ratan Tata, Aditya Birla, Shahrukh Khan, Operah Winfrey, Thomas Edison etc. They are no different people, they also have 2 eyes, one nose, hands, legs, brain etc everything what we have. Yet these people are successful. God has made no discrimination, it's just they give 100% of their passion, dedication, commitment to the work they love and achieve it. We also have brain and desire to get what we want and to add your name in the list of those successful people, you just have to follow these 10 steps and success will be yours.

1. Failure: A stepping stone towards success.

It's not necessary that to become successful we have to fail but I just want to say that failure gives us experience; we learn from them what to repeat next time and where to take a step back. To reach the ladder of success, failure is the first step. It makes us stronger and wiser. Don't fear of failure, face it rather embrace it with your brilliant smile and cross every bridge of failure to reach your goal. Rest everything is described in earlier chapter.

> *"I can accept failure, everyone fails at something. But I can't accept not trying."*
> *—Michael Jordan*

2. Attitude

Attitude is nothing but a habit which is repeated again and again and that habit can be a positive or negative. Attitude is a point of view about a situation. Attitude comprises of what you think, what you do and what you feel. No matter what situation you are in, you always have certain thoughts about it. You also have an emotional response to it and you behave accordingly. Attitude is a mental habit that filters how you perceive the world around you and also the actions and behaviors you take in response. You cannot control what happens to you but you can control your attitude towards it. Don't let any situation master you; in fact make your attitude so good and rigid that you master every situation and get the ball in your court.

"Whenever you're in a conflict with someone, there is one factor that can make the difference between damaging your relationship and deepening it. That factor is attitude."

—William James

STORY: It is the little things that make big difference.

There was a man taking a morning walk at or the beach. He saw that along with the morning tide came hundreds of starfish and when the tide receded, they were left behind and with the morning sun rays, they would die. The tide was fresh and the starfish were alive. The man took a few steps, picked one and threw it into the water. He did that repeatedly. Right behind him there was another person who couldn't understand what this man was doing. He caught up with him and asked, "What are you doing? There are hundreds of starfish. How many can you help? What difference does it make?" This man did not reply, took two more steps, picked up another one, threw it into the water, and said, "It makes a difference to this one."

What do we learn from this story? 2 mindsets can be developed. One which think that its worth wasting time doing such actions as it doesn't make any difference (negative attitude) while a positive attitude gives us an inner feeling of care, contemplates us to think about those starfish and take a positive step ahead to give life to someone. Edward de Bono in his book, Tactics: The Art and Science of Success, writes—you don't have to value success. But if you do want to be successful, then there are two attitudes. The first is the passive attitude which tells you that there is nothing you can do except wait for luck or pray for the right temperature and talent. The second is the positive attitude, which tells you that there are things you can do that will make a difference.

> *"To be upset over what you don't have is to waste what you do have."*
> *—Ken S. Keyes*

> *"Our attitude toward life determines life's attitude towards us."*
> *—John N. Mitchell*

May be you've heard this or read this quote and you really want to change your attitude towards life. However you may not have any idea about how to go about it. Actually, attitude is the driving force in our life and without right attitude, our life becomes directionless. Without right attitude there remains no difference between us and animals. It is attitude which distinguishes humans from other animals. Attitude is kind of one's expression towards life and others. It may be positive, negative, indifferent or some thing else. A positive attitude is very important for generating a successful land satisfied life. Right attitude can be developed by adopting certain things like:

i. **Change your thinking:** We and our surrounding create an environment around us. What we do, what we think and what we feel are reciprocated by the universe in the same way we give to it. If we spread joy, happiness we get the same feeling from others and if we give anger, frustration and hate to others; people will not love us rather hate us. And to change our environment, we have to change our thinking. Why everybody always says to us, "be Positive" because by being positive we can change our thinking, our actions and our life.

    Identify what is happening to you. What makes you feel good and fills you with joy and excitement. Every time you feel good, wait for some time and ponder what that was and then stick to do that thing. Happiness fills joy within us and creates a positive attitude by which we will do positive actions.

ii. **Change your actions:** Actions speak more than words. Do certain acts for goodwill of yourself, your family and friends. Spread happiness by giving away the things what other wants like help some one in lifting the luggage, help the blind person in crossing the road, help your father in business, help yourself to understand who you are and nurture yourself with positive feeds.

Every morning you wake up promise to yourself that today I am going to make at least one person happy and bring smile on his face. Today I'll help the needy one. Today I'll complete my pending task. Don't just think in your mind; convert that potential energy in your mind to kinetic energy through your hands and do such good deeds.

iii. **Be Patient:** Developing a positive attitude is not an overnight process. Attitude is developed by repeating a certain habit again and again. If you want to develop an attitude of good listener, start listening to your parents quietly and calmly, start listening to other's views without interrupting them, speak only if required and practice it daily. Sooner or later you'll find that you're a good listener now. In the same way develop attitude of positive thing by repeating mantras, positive affirmations like I am the best, I can do it. Practice it daily.

iv. **Be Ready to Learn:** Nobody is perfect and if you think you don't have anything to learn from this life then you are living with a wrong attitude. Actually every one of us can learn so many things everyday if we keep our senses alert. Even if you are brilliant and you have never failed in your life, there are many things to learn from this life. Therefore, whether you are at work, home or anywhere else, be ready to learn and you'll feel satisfied.

v. **Principles of Changing Attitude:** If you want to improve or change your attitude then you have to integrate following principles into your life. It is not a glass of milk which can be drunk at one shot, it is like learning any foreign language which takes some time to learn and adopt and use it in our daily life so as we can be accustomed to it.

1. Love and Self-esteem: Love yourself and others without any limitations and expectations. Until and unless you won't love anything, you would not feel good about it. Don't change anyone according to you. Love them the way they are. If you can truly do this, the world is at your feet and with your love you'll be able to attract all good things to you. Let your mind become free of taking any love; fill your mind to give love to others.

Always keep in mind that nobody in this world is like you, you are unique. You are God's gift. God has given you a life to make it worth by doing such good actions and feel good about it. And when we are happy, it ignites a blow of energy, joy and excitement within us and with this energy, we can create miracles.

2. Forgiveness: In our lifetime everybody must have gone through certain tragedy which is residing in our sub conscious mind. At regular breaks we think of it because someone might have hurt you and you can't forget his/her words and when our mind thinks over it, we drain all our mental energy to that and fills ourselves with negative emotions. We often feel guilty, angry or just the feeling of hating everybody. What we have to do in such situation is "Let your past go." All what had happened with you because of your mistake or because of anyone's fault, it is just the past now. Forgive it, forgive everyone and specially forgive yourself.

Whatever the issue may be, a small tragedy or life shattering situation, you just have to move on. Don't take the burden of your past on your shoulders, fall them off and release yourself. Always remember life is in now, forget the past, dead can't be made alive. You can't do anything over changing the past but what you can do is forgive every person in your life and take positive actions to build your life and make a difference now. By realizing and forgiving everybody, you'll release yourself.

3. Awareness: Take out some time for yourself, sit alone and think about what you speak, what you feel and what sort of actions you take in your daily routine life. Do your actions play any important role in manifestation of your life? Do your actions give you an edge over others to be different and smart? Are you aware that everybody is happy with the way you speak to them or the words you use while speaking? Have you ever thought what your actual role is?

First let yourself make aware of what you are, who you are; rest of the world is secondary. By taking some time to examine your lives, your own needs, your own behavior; you are not only closely related to yourself but you'll get answers for your questions and learn from your past success and mistakes. You should be aware of what is going on in your mind and heart. Find out is it you who controls your mind or is it the mind who controls you?

To a disciple who always seeks answers from his master, he says "You have within yourself the answer to every question you propose; if you only know how to look for it."

STORY

A king and his troops were going through a forest. The King saw an old man cutting trees. Taking pity on him, he asked the Minister to give that old man an acre of sandalwood trees. The Minister took care of that instantly.

A couple of years later, the King and his troops were again passing through the forest and in fact, they were passing by the area where there were sandalwood trees given away to that old man.

The king noticed that most of the sandalwood trees were gone and in one corner the old man was there. He was burning a couple of sandalwood trees. Upon talking to him, the Minister found out that he was burning those trees to collect coal BECAUSE that is what does—sells coal and makes money.

This is a simple story about awareness. Sometimes we have riches right in front of our eyes but if we can't see them as such, they are not riches to us.

4. Gratitude: There are certain people who always criticize for what they have; they either blame God or some other people for their present condition. Such kinds of people never accompany joy in their life as they have already filled themselves with jealousy, resentment, lacking etc. Do you also want to add your name in such list of people? If No; then always be grateful for what you have. Rather than focusing your energy on empty part of your life, move your focus to the life which is fully alive and full of happiness.

Feel grateful that you are not suffering from cancer, feel grateful that you are a literate person, feel grateful that you have your own vehicle, feel grateful that you can sit in McDonald and eat pizza. Because there are crores of people in the world who don't even have a shelter, one time food to eat and clothes to wear. Whatever the situation is, always be grateful and thank everybody to be a part of your life.

5. Honesty: Honesty is that mirror which shows you who you are and what you really want. When you're lying to someone, the mirror will reflect and it will give you cheated and wrong results. You'll get what you'll row. When you lie about yourself or pretend to be someone what you are not then the person to whom you're cheating is YOU. If you had done any mistake then admit it and be honest to yourself. Initially people might dislike you for what you did, your friends might leave you for lying to them but you remain true to yourself and it gives self satisfaction and eventually when everybody gets to know a new YOU within yourself, people will try to connect themselves with you and will support you in your need.

6. Be Positive / Take Positive Actions: Your actions depict what you feel and think. If today you're doing the work you love, it means you've filled yourself with positive energy and if you're angry with someone and yelling at somebody; it shows what sort of personality you are. If I say you to think about Mother Teresa for a moment, you'll imagine a picture of a lady wearing white dress who is helping poor and needy people. And if I say you to think about Hitler, a different scenario will come up in your mind about a man who wears pent shirt, a cap and a stick in his hand, who is cruel and brutal to others. What I mean to say is their actions depict what they feel and think.

Same way your actions predict yourself. Take a control over what you do and feel positive about everything you face in your daily routine life. It is like a coin, if you're facing negative side of coin; always remember the other side is positive. Accept every challenge coming towards you and make a commitment to yourself that you'll turn every worse situation in you favor through positive thinking and positive actions.

7. Taking Responsibility: This is a very important principle. As we grew up; we become mature and we start taking our own decisions which means we are responsible for what is happening with us. But there are some people who always blame others and the circumstances, always criticize for what they have and blame their destiny for their present situation. Once we stop blaming others and accept that we are responsible for everything happening to us; it will give us relief to feel in a better position and to move forward with new zeal, enthusiasm and energy.

We need to learn from our mistakes because experience comes from learning and learning comes from mistakes we did. Doing a mistake is not bad repeating same mistake again and again is wrong. We need to learn from it and apply new strategies with new ideas at new steps. Always remember if or relationships are not going well with others then we need to examine ourselves and our behavior. Analyze yourself as if what is that thing which is creating a boundary between you and your dear one and try to break that wall.

And when we stop taking responsibility and deny for any mistake done by us, then
- people will loose faith
- you are not trustworthy
- you fail in relationship
- your growth will become stagnant
- unable to take any decision
- fear of doing any task
- people will not like talking to you

8. Be open and trustworthy: Let yourself go and be open for everything whatever is coming to you. Let go all the fear and welcome the whole universe with open arms and trust yourself more than anyone. Remember there is nobody like you and you are unique. Keep your doors open for every opportunity and be worthy enough o bring everything what you deserve.

3. Focus

Focus has been well defined as the ability to embrace a worthwhile goal and then employ all of your powers for the achievement of that goal.

Have you ever seen that when the magnifying glass is moving, it can light a paper? Probably NO! But what if you focus and hold the magnifying glass in front of sunny rays, the paper will light up. That is the power of concentration and focus. It all depends on us whether we want to achieve our goal or not. If we are not sure of what exactly we want then we may get distracted from our surroundings and give all such kind of excuses for which we are not able to fulfill our dream and reach our goal. But we really have passion for what we want; we have to give our 100% focus to it. It doesn't matter whether you're a soccer player or a student of history; you need to focus on the task at hand. There are too many distractions around but if you are committed and focused, nothing can stop you from succeeding.

Let me share with you a story. A man was traveling and stopped at an intersection. He asked an elderly man, "Where does this road take me?" The elderly person asked, "Where do you want to go?" The man replied, "I don't know." The elderly person said, "Then take any road, what difference does it make?" How true! When we don't know where we are going, any road will take us there.

If we are not focused at where we want to reach in our life, we are just like animals that are roaming here and there; eat what they want and die whenever their time is over. We are not animals; we are human beings. God has given us a brain (a tiny machine which can do wonders and miracles) by which we can focus on our purpose of life and then put all your efforts to fulfill it. As rightly said by Swami Vivekananda, "Take up one idea. make that one idea your life—think of it, dream of it, and live on that idea. Let the brain, muscles, nerves, every part of your body, be full of that idea and just leave any other idea alone. This is the way to success, which is way great spiritual giants are produced."

STORY

An ancient Indian sage was teaching his disciples the art of archery. He put a wooden bird as the target and asked them to aim at the eye of the bird. The first disciple was asked to describe what he saw. He said, "I see the trees, the branches, the leaves, the sky, the bird and its eye . . ." The sage asked this disciple to wait. Then he asked the second disciple the same question and he replied, "I only see the eye of the bird." The sage said, "Very good, then shoot." The arrow went straight and hit the eye of the bird.

What is the moral of the story?
Unless we focus, we cannot achieve our goal. It is hard to focus and concentrate, but it is a skill that can be learned.

Just remember one thing, don't concentrate on how bad you are or how incapable you are to do any task because if you concentrate on what you can't do, you'll waste your time and energy for what you can actually do. Just focus and think of how powerful you are how you can contribute to this planet and then you can see the difference within you.

You are the Director of your life. You choose where to put the focus. Your focus shapes your life. So if you want to redesign your life; reshape your focus. And while focusing; take one task at hand and then put all your energy to it, don't try to sit on 2 boats at one time.

> *"The best advice I ever came across on the subject of concentration is: Wherever you are, be there. When you work, work; you play, play. Don't mix the two."*
>
> *—Jim Rohn*

4. Believe in yourself

Belief means trust/faith. It's only the belief of one person that can turn a rock into GOD. It's the belief which can convert the impossible to possible. Belief is that magic which can create miracles and wonders in the world.

> *"The only thing that stands between a man and what wants from life is often merely the will to try it and faith to believe it is possible."*
>
> *—Richard Devos*

STORY

Once upon a time, there was an eagle that grew up with a group of chickens. He thought of himself as a chicken too, enjoying a routine life the same as everybody else. His master was very angry when trying various methods to get him to fly, but he couldn't.

Finally, one day, his master brought him to the top of a mountain and threw him down the cliff. He was surprised, sad, and confused. He thought, "Oh God, my master is going to kill me, I don't want to die." While he was struggling, he opened up his wings and, all of the sudden; he felt a strong force that took him up. The more he extended his wings, the more he could rise. Well, he started to fly.

For the first time, he saw lots of different things: blue skies, white clouds, green trees, and gray. He felt freedom. Since then, he could never go back to the same life as a chicken—he could not stop flying.

Don't waste your time in doing the things what others think about you or tell you to do. There will be always a group of people who will direct you or criticize you for what you're doing. And if you listen to them

- You will deviate from your path.
- You will do the things what your mind does not allow you to do.

- You will not be satisfied from your work.
- You will think that still something is missing.
- Eventually you'll feel frustrated and irritated.
- Your behavior will change and you will act in a manner which you are actually not.
- And ultimately you'll become a different personality.

So you have to stop listening to such people then and there. Believing in yourself is all about being sure that you are going to do whatever you want even if others were against you.

> *"Believe in yourself and there will come a day when others will have no choice but to believe with you."*
> *—Cynthia Kersey*

There will be a time when things will not be according to your wish, a long queue of challenges will stand in front of you, lots of disappointing people to let you down and that's when you have to tell yourself that I believe myself and I know what I can do and prove all of them wrong by constantly keeping yourself in right direction while facing all challenges and prove the world that you are worth it. You just need to keep certain things in mind to fill yourself with belief.

1. **Stop listening to others:** You are not born to please others but to live the life the way you want. There will always be some people who will command over you and rule you but keep in mind that master key is with you and you'll open the lock whenever you want it. Do the

things what your heart and mind says and stop bothering about others. Erase the fear from your mind about, "Sabse bada h rog, kya kahenge log."

2. **Change your thinking about yourself:** A constant thinking of self defeating assumptions obviously puts you in the place of believing you cannot succeed. The moment you get such vibrations in your mind, direct your mind to stop then and there. Because nobody in this world will know you better except YOU. What is already done is just the past, now you're a different personality and move on with the attitude of "Yes, I can do it."

3. **Identify your potential:** Sit silent for sometime and do a self analysis and ask yourself what are you best at, what is that thing that gives you an edge over others. You can even ask your friends and family members to tell your potential and then put all your energy to work on it and make it your strong axe.

   "You must do your thing rather than trying to fit your square talents into your round hole."

   —Marcus Buckhingham

4. **Challenge yourself:** In order to do this you should establish a list of items that you are thoroughly convinced that you are able to do. Once you do this, you are able to start tackling

each task one by one. Sooner you'll find that you are able to do much more than you have imagined that you could. And you'll discover that the list you initially created is getting smaller and smaller. This will help you establish the ability to believe in yourself that you do offer something to yourself and be true to you.

5. **Try even if you can't:** While challenging yourself there will be a time when you're not able to perform or fail but you need not to worry. Promise yourself that you will try your best at any opportunity that comes to your way. It doesn't matter how many times you've failed; what matters is you still try.

"Take the first step in faith. You don't have to see the whole staircase, just take the first step."
                    —Dr. Martin Luther King Jr.

6. **Be Confident:** And of course be confident over what you're doing.

5. Passion, Dedication & Commitment

Do you want to fulfill your dreams? Remember one thing, dreams are fulfilled of only those who only see, hear and feel the music of passion; those who become deaf, dumb and blind to anything else they see which is not in contrast to their dream. To achieve the goal everyone adopts different methods. To some hard work is necessary while to some concentration is required. Some believe in networking and some in information. But to reach your goal utmost requirement is of passion. Passion is a deep connection to an idea, a strong bond which creates a feeling of desire. It contains elements of both dedication and commitment but is not limited to them.

Passion should be of such cadre that you don't like anything else which deviate you from your path. Weather its morning or evening, day or night; your mind knows only your goal and is passionate about it. People of such nature are not worried about their surroundings, they are happy when they do the work they love and get unhappy while doing other stuff. They don't care what people say about them or what they think about them; they just know only one thing and that is passion to reach their goals and passion to fulfill their dreams.

It's not necessary that you always have all the facilities or guidance to move on the path but if your vision is clear in your mind; such materialistic things don't affect you. It's only your energy, your concentration and your focus which brings spark in you and takes you to your course.

> *"When you really want something to happen, the whole universe conspires so that your wish comes true."*
> —*Paulo Coelho*

> *"When you have a great and difficult task, something perhaps almost impossible, if you only work a little at a time, everyday a little, suddenly the work will finish itself."*
> —*Unknown*

One of the most important ingredients in manifesting our dreams is dedication and commitment. Without them, all your energy put in to achieve your goal will go in vain. It takes commitment if we are going to achieve or complete something fairly big. Writing a book for example needs dedication and commitment. It is a joyous task to those who loves writing but then they also spare some time and make it worth reading. Always remember, you'll get what you'll give. Set your mind by clearly defining your vision, and just pour hard work, passion, dedication and commitment to nurture your world and get a fruitful result. And when you continue doing this then there will be co incidences, chances and lucky breaks that will speed you along your path to your goal.

There is a difference between interest and commitment. When you're interested in doing something, you do it only when circumstances permit. When you're committed to something, you accept no excuses; only results. Commitment comes from the heart, and when you do commit and take baby steps towards your goal; your life will open up. Until you discover your "fir within" you will remain condemned to a life only endured, not lived; to delicacies only tasted, not devoured; to joys only imagined, not experienced.

So what will you do today? Crash on the couch after work, or take a few small steps towards living the life of your dreams?

6. Perseverance

Perseverance is the continued effort to do or achieve something despite difficulties, failure or opposition. Let me ask you a question. How many times you've failed while doing something or progressing towards your goal? How many times you have retried to again keep your full energy to reach the destination? Your answer may be once, twice, ten times or thousand times. It might have taken 1 year, 2 year, 5, and 10 or may be 20 years. But your actual answer should be, "I've fallen down and get up, again fall down and get up until I reach my goal. No matter how many times I tried or no matter how long did it took, what matters me most is that I achieved my goal by my continuous efforts keeping patience in my heart and mind."

> *"I've missed more than 9000 shots in my career. I've lost almost 300 games, 26 times; I've been trusted to take the game winning shot and missed. I've failed over and over and over again in my life. And that is why I succeed."*
>
> *—Michael Jordan*
> *(Olympic Gold medalist Basketball player)*

All those at the top have the same character trait in common: perseverance. The history books are full of examples of people who succeed as a result of never giving up. The biography of great people proves that persistence pays off. Perseverance is required for successful achievement. The most successful people in all fields never give up. Persistence and perseverance will allow you to succeed also. No one achieves total success without going through setbacks, hardships and opposition. Perseverance means to hold out and remain steadfast until the end.

But when people don't get what they want, they get frustrated, irritated, start shouting at others, feels distressed and start living alone or show their anger to some pity one. When things are not working, you need to back off and start fresh. Stay cool, stay calm and imagine the end in your conscious mind and your sub conscious mind will take over and direct your actions. As Thomas A. Edison has rightly said "Our greatest weakness lies in giving up. The most certain way to succeed is always to try just one more time.

Be like a postage stamp and stick to one thing until you get there. There will be bad time when bad things happen to you; you experience disappointment or setbacks, you'll be hurt by something someone said. Let perseverance carry you through pain, distress and pressure. Perseverance is the only thing that can turn defeat and failure into success and victory. If you fail, start over changing your methods, learn from your mistakes and then try a new approach. Once you convince yourself that there has to be a way to do what you want; you become unstoppable. Believing that a problem can't be solved makes it unsolvable. Believing that solutions are possible attracts the right answer to you.

"Perseverance is the hard work you do after you get tired of doing the hard work you already did."

— *Newt Gingrich*

"Look at a stone cutter hammering away at his rock, perhaps a hundred times without as much as a crack showing in it. Yet at the hundred and first blow it will split in two, and I know it was not the last blow that did it, but all that had gone before."

— *Jacob A. Riis*

7. Love Your Work

Every person in this world is doing something; every individual is working for something, every person wakes up early and get himself ready for his work let it be a clerk going for duty, a sales person going for a call, a doctor getting ready for an operation, a housewife making food for family, a pilot to take off or a kid going to school. Everybody's task and work is fixed; everybody's schedule is set. But do these people really love their work? When they are going out from their home, do they have a smile on their face? Do they feel excited about their job? Do they feel special about themselves for what they're doing?

Once asked by a school teacher that what she does. She replied, "I am a teacher and I educate children." Same question was asked by another teacher and she replied, "I am a teacher and I help students in learning the things." Again the same question was asked by another teacher and she said, "I make them learn how to live or rather how to lead their life; I make them a good human being by put in all good habits, etiquettes, respect and manners."

This is a real sense of belongingness or love towards their job. All three ladies were doing same job but the third one loves what she does.

> *"Choose a job you love, and you will never have to work a day in your life."*
> —*Confucius*

Everyday we hear about people making radical career changes. Someone is not happy with his work, someone is not getting pleasure doing it, while someone is not satisfied and for some this is not their cup of tea. Every now and then people change their job. Sometimes life hits you in the head with brick. Don't loose faith. You've got to find what you truly love. Your work is going to fill large part of your life, and the only way to be truly satisfied is to do what you believe is great work. And the only way to do great work is to love what you do. If you haven't found it yet keep looking. Don't settle. Your time is limited so don't waste it living someone else's life. Don't let the noise of other's opinions drown out your own inner voice. And most important; have the courage to follow your heart and intuition. In order to be really good and successful at something, we have to enjoy doing it. If you don't, often times you'll find yourself not being very successful at it.

"I never worked a day in my life. It's not work when you love what you're doing."
—*David Shakarian*

The question is not "How can I get the job I love?" but "How can I love the job I have?" Take some time to really think about what you do and what you love. Then ask yourself, "How this job can be done differently because I am doing it?" Your perspective plays a huge role in personal satisfaction and sense of well being. Be aware of what you're doing because the awareness can lead you to greater job satisfaction, increased sense of well being and a little more control over what you are, rather than just going along with the ride. For some it may be the time for a change and if it is so; don't be afraid of it. Change isn't necessarily bad, it's just different. For the rest of you, take a look around; you may find you've got a great view.

You're worth here. Ask yourself and find out who you are, where you're good at. Don't get a feeling of fear and resentment instead engage your head over them? Dialog with them; journal your way through them. Listen to your inner voice and get in touch with deeper part of yourself you've been wishing. You're not here to settle; to fit in, or to work for money; you're here to shine.

So from now love your job because when work is pleasure, life is joy and if you feel that your work is duty, life is slavery. The way you love your job can be a lot more interesting and telling than the job itself. Don't tell me what you do, tell me why? So now tell me what's your work love story?

8. Self-Discipline

> **"Self discipline begins with the mastery of your thoughts. If you don't control what you think, you can't control what you do. Simply, self discipline enables you to think first and act afterward."**
>
> **—Napolean Hill**

STORY: The Elephant and the Fly

A disciple and his teacher were walking through the forest. The disciple was disturbed by the fact that his mind was in constant unrest.

He asked his teacher: "Why most people's minds are restless, and only a few possess a calm mind? What can one do to still the mind?"

The teacher looked at the disciple, smiled and said: "I will tell you a story. An elephant was standing and picking leaves from a tree. A small fly came, flying and buzzing near his ear. The elephant waved it away with his long ears. Then the fly came again, and the elephant waved it away once more."

This was repeated several times. Then the elephant asked the fly: "Why are you so restless and noisy? Why can't you stay for a while in one place?"

The fly answered: "I am attracted to whatever I see, hear or smell. My five senses, and everything that happens around me, pull me constantly in all directions, and I cannot resist them. What is your secret? How can you stay so calm and still?"

The elephant stopped eating and said: "My five senses do not rule my attention. I am in control of my attention, and I can direct it wherever I want. This helps me to get immersed in whatever I do, and therefore, keep my mind focused and calm. Now that I am eating, I am completely immersed in eating. In this way, I can enjoy my food and chew it better. I control my attention, and not the other way around, and this helps me stay peaceful."

Upon hearing these words, the disciple's eyes opened wide, and a smile appeared on his face. He looked at his teacher and said: "I understand! My mind will be in constant unrest, if my five senses and whatever is happening in the world around me are in control of it. On the other hand, if I am in command of my five senses, able to disregard sense impressions, my mind would become calm, and I will be able to disregard its restlessness."

"Yes, that's right," answered the teacher," The mind is restless and goes wherever the attention is. Control your attention, and you control your mind."

Self discipline involves acting according to what you think instead of how you feel in the moment. Often it involves sacrificing the pleasure and thrill of the moment for what matters most in life. Philosophy of self discipline can be best explained by an analogy. Self discipline is like muscle. The more you train it, the stronger you become. The way to build self discipline is analogous to using progressive weight training to build muscle. This means lifting weights that are close to your limits. Note that you lift weights that are within your ability to lift. You push your muscles until they fail and then you rest.

Similarly, the basic method to build self discipline is to tackle challenges that you can successfully accomplish but which are near your limit. Neither this doesn't mean trying something nor failing at it everyday nor does it mean staying within your comfort zone. You will gain no strength trying to lift a weight that you can carry nor will you gain strength lifting weights that are too light for you. You must start with weights / challenges that are within your current ability to lift but which are near your limit.

> *"Discipline really means our ability to get ourselves to do things when we don't want."*
> —*Arden Mahlberg*

Thus by adopting self discipline and regularly practicing it; you will align yourself with your inner peace and you can be peace with the rest of the world. If your thoughts are under your control; you become strong and firm. So whenever you face any problem or challenge, don't react instantly or jump or feel fade or sad; apply the game of STOP-WAIT-GO. Whenever we are standing in front of a challenge, don't fight but stop as it is giving a red signal to you, wait for some time, contemplate on your problem while the light goes yellow. Think of the alternatives you can pertain to solve the problem and when light goes green, adopt the best method to solve your problem and go towards it so that you get fruitful result and also an experience of solving a problem adopting self discipline. By doing this, good habits will develop. The ability to concentrate and to control the thoughts will be strengthened.

As Stephen R. Covey once wrote, "the undisciplined are slaved to moods, appetites and passions." You are no more slave to your moods, you are able to control your mind and direct your thoughts in a particular way to develop a habit that will help you to live life a better way in the long term. You are a winner if you conquer yourself.

> *"Rule your mind or it will rule you."*
> —*Horace*

9. Be deaf to criticism

When you are proceeding towards your goal, there will be certain group of people who will discourage you in spite of motivating you and will distract you from your path. Such people say some common lines to you, "This is impossible", "You can't do it", "You are not eligible for it", "Just leave it", "Why you're trying to do it again and again?", "You can't achieve this." Such people themselves don't have any sense of being motivated or achieving something with a vision in their eyes. Neither do they achieve anything nor do they let it happen for others. Always remember, when one judge or criticize another person, it says nothing about that person; it merely say something about one's own need to be critical.

STORY

Once upon a time there was a bunch of tiny frogs who arranged a running competition.

The goal was to reach the top of a very high tower. A big crowd had gathered around the tower to see the race and cheer on the contestants. The race began. Honestly, No one in crowd really believed that the tiny frogs would reach the top of the tower. You heard statements such as, "Oh, WAY too difficult!!", "They will NEVER make it to the top.", "Not a chance that they will succeed. The tower is too high!"

The tiny frogs began collapsing one by one except for those, who in a fresh tempo, were climbing higher and higher. The crowd continued to yell, "It is too difficult!!! No one will make it!" More tiny frogs got tired and gave up. But ONE continued higher and higher and higher. This one wouldn't give up! At the end everyone else had given up climbing the tower. Except for the one tiny frog that, after a big effort, was the only one who reached the top! THEN all of the other tiny frogs naturally wanted to know how this one frog managed to do it? A contestant asked the tiny frog how he had found the strength to succeed and reach the goal. It turned out that the winner was DEAF!!!!

The wisdom of this story is never listen to other people's tendencies to be negative or pessimistic because they take your most wonderful dreams and wishes away from you—the ones you have in your heart!! Always think of the power words you have because everything you hear and read will affect your actions!!! Therefore always be POSITIVE and above all be DEAF when people tell you that you cannot fulfill your dreams!!

At every stage of your life, you'll face such situation and people what that frog was facing and at that time you have to be deaf to criticism and move forward as if you don't care who the king is.

> *"Don't mind criticism. If it is untrue, disregard it; if unfair, keep from irritation; if it is ignorant, smile; if it is justified, it is not criticism; learn from it."*
>
> *—Unknown*

Never bother about others, walk like you are the king or walk like you don't bother who is the king. Whatever comes to you, take it on a positive note and as Eleavon Roosevelt say, "Do what you feel in your heart to be right. You'll be criticized anyway." Believe in what you're doing and immerse yourself fully into it.

10. Never Give Up

> *"Our greatest glory is not in ever failing,*
> *but in rising up every time we fail."*
> — *Ralph Waldo Emerson*

At some point in the various journeys we embark on in our lives, we get to a part where we feel like giving up. Sometime we give up before we even start and other times we give up just before we are about to make that huge break through that we have been putting so much effort to achieve. I don't say that giving up is a bad quality of a person but giving up without even trying to achieve something is not a good quality for sure. I believe, "Not Giving up Does Not Assures Your Success or Win All the Time, but Giving up Always Guarantees Your Failure and Loss." As Dr. Martin Luther King Jr. says—"Take the first step in faith. You don't have to see the whole staircase, just take the first step."

Whenever you feel like giving up, just remember following points:

1. **Everything is Possible:** The only valid excuse you have to give up is that you are dead. As long as you are alive you have the choice to keep trying until you finally succeed. So wait for the correct time to achieve something, failure in

present does not represent failure always. It is possible to succeed in future if one tries his best.

2. **Be Practical:** I remember when I was kid; I use to play Mario Game and let me tell you it took 5 trials to clear even the first stage. So when one cannot clear a virtual game in first attempt, then real life difficulties are far more difficult than those games. Then how can one assume to achieve everything in life in very first time.

3. **Be Strong:** You are string enough to fight over what you want. One little set back is not enough to stop you neither 10 or 100 or 1000.

4. **Improve Yourself:** Every time you fail. Every time you commit mistakes; learn from it because experience will come only after by doing something right or wrong but do it. Improve your skills and actions in a positive way to build up a new personality who can now achieve his/her goal.

5. **Believe in your dreams:** Don't listen to others; nobody else knows you better than you. You know who you are; and always be confident about it and feel proud about your dreams. There are people who don't have any dreams and are just living their life. You are lucky that at least you have the capacity to achieve and succeed. Don't sell yourself short. Don't let any one destroy your dreams.

"One of the lessons that I grew up with was to always stay true to yourself and never let what somebody else says and distracts you from your goals. And so when I hear about negative and false attitude, I really don't invest any energy in them because I know who I am."

—*Michalle Obama*

6. **You are very close:** Often when you feel like you want to give up and you are about to give up; you are so close to making a huge breakthrough.

   "Don't be discouraged. It's often the last key in the bunch that opens the lock."

   —*Unknown*

7. **Be Grateful:** As Mark Victor Hansen says, "Always be grateful for your problems, for they stimulate an "I-Can-Solve-It" attitude."

5th Meeting

The sun is about to rise but before rising it has sent its light to wake up the people. A cool breeze is blowing which soothes your mind completely. Everywhere there was greenery and people in their track suits were running, laughing, meditating and exercising according to their need. Amidst all the people, at one corner of the garden where the grass was still wet, Nysha maam was sitting silently and calmly with her closed eyes.

She was wearing black pajama and white sleeveless top and her hairs were clutched in a pony tail. Her face was radiant and illuminating as if one more small sun is on the earth.

But I don't understand what she was doing all alone sitting idle and I even don't understand how come such large number of people can take the pains of waking up early in the morning, get ready with their pajamas and walk in the garden. I mean morning bed sleep is much better than this silly walk in the garden.

And to my shock what I saw there was unbelievable; my mouth remained wide open with broad bulging eyes when I saw Rajveer coming there and he stood beside Nysha maam.

Rajveer's face was shaggy and I can tell by seeing his face that he is there only after giving lots of curses and abusive words to come in the garden early in the morning. He was still in his sleep and I think he hasn't washed his face even.

He was standing quite waiting for Nysha maam to open to her eyes but she was sitting calmly and didn't realize that Rajveer has come.

After a minute or two, Rajveer's patience broke and he said, "Good morning Nysha Ji."

Nysha maam slowly opened her eyes, looked above at Rajveer and said, "Very goog morning Rajveer."

"So you're here; I thought you wouldn't come," Nysha maam chuckled.

Whenever she smiles, I get mesmerized with it. She is really adorable. She has a killing smile.

Today Nysha maam had called him in the garden early in the morning; may be to teach something new.

"Initially I thought I wouldn't come; but soon your face comes up I my mind and then my past and then I thought if I had to get rid of it, let's take some pain to wake up early and I'm here," Rajveer said briskly.

"Come, sit next to me Rajveer," Nysha maam said.

Rajveer sat down on the wet grass beside her and was thinking what he will do now and why Nysha maam had called him here.

"Are you feeling good?" she asked.

Rajveer's eyes were roaming around to look at the view of the garden, wet and green grass spread all over, some people were walking, some were sitting and breathing in a mysterious way and the strange part is today he is also amongst those people.

"Yes all good," Rajveer replied half heartedly.

"Of course not, how can be I good when you called me here early morning," his mind was saying.

"Wow, what a cool and soothing breeze," Nysha maam said cheerfully.

Rajveer nodded and said nothing.

Nysha maam soon sensed Rajveer and his mood of not so feeling good over there and she said, "I know Rajveer you are missing your morning bed sleep but now as if you're here; forget that sleep and look at the beauty of nature and try to enjoy this particular moment."

"Yes yes Nysha Ji, now I'm awake," Rajveer responded while opening his eyes wide enough and try to comfort him of missing his morning bed sleep.

Both Nysha maam and Rajveer sat cross legged and put their hands straight on knees wherein there thumb and first finger were touching each other.

"Now close your eyes for 2 minutes and take a deep breathe in, hold on for a second and breathe out. Again hold for a second, breathe in, hold and breathe out," Nysha maam said while doing above act of breathing.

Rajveer also followed what she was instructing.

After 2 minutes both of them opened their eyes.

"Everyday after waking up, do this exercise for 5 minute and I promise you'll actually feel good," Nysha maam said.

"Can I ask you one question please?" Rajveer requested.

"Yes of course."

"What is the use of this exercise?" Rajveer asked.

"Firstly this will clear your mind and calms it and secondly make some space for new positive thoughts," Nysha maam answered.

"Positive thoughts?" Rajveer dazed.

"Yes it's the way you think about everything," she further clarified, "like suppose you always say you're an empty idiot box, life is no more fun, you're alone and everything like that; you've actually filled your mind with these negative thoughts which can be removed by doing certain exercises and then you can be all new man with lots of positivity."

Rajveer said nothing but was trying to understand the phenomenon of deleting some thoughts from his mind and filling it again with some positive ones.

It seems as if Rajveer had to empty one barrel of impure water and refill it with pure water but doing the same act with the mind is not easy.

"And for doing this, firstly you have to be positive," Nysha maam insisted.

"And how I'm supposed to have positive thinking?" Rajveer asked solicitously.

"Change the way you look at something or think about it, change your perspective," she said.

"Seek positivity in every small or big thing. Like for an half filled glass of water; negative thinking will say it is half empty while positive thinking will say it is half full. That's it; apply the same principle on everything," she explained.

"Now I'm getting it. That's why you've said little stress is good for me. That is your positive thinking towards stress, right?" Rajveer said.

"Yes, now you got my point," Nysha maam smiled.

"And now I'll tell you some of the techniques to adopt this positive thinking in your life forever," she said.

"What are these techniques?" Rajveer asked while lifting up his eyebrows.

"But before that you've to promise me that you'll follow them certainly. If not all; but few of them. These are very simple one and trust me it will definitely pay you in future," Nysha maam said firmly and put forward her hand to get promise.

"Hmmm . . . (Thinking what to do) OK if you say so then I promise to do them," Rajveer agreed and hold Nysha maam's hand and shook it.

"Great, Thank you for saying yes," Nysha maam smiled.

"Why thank you? If you're doing so much for me then I guess I can do this little effort for myself; right?" Rajveer said.

Nysha maam nodded.

"First one is positive affirmations where in you have say positive statements to yourself like I am the best, I can do it, I am a winner, Today is my day, I do the work I love, I am a very happy person and so on. Say it standing in front of the mirror and repeat all such statements. Secondly do some exercise including physical, mental and spiritual," Nysha maam said.

"I thought exercise was limited only to physical one. It's totally new for me that there are mental or spiritual exercises too." Rajveer said doubtfully.

"Don't worry I'll explain you everything," Nysha maam said.

"Third is meditation and yoga," Nysha maam was about to continue but Rajveer intervened and said, "Oh yes yes I know this; it's all about what Ramdev Baba teaches on T.V."

"Great, at least you know this one," Nysha maam tittered

"Fourth is visualization," she said.

"Again, I don't know this. What is it now?" Rajveer baffled and asked.

"Everything that happens in this world occurs twice. Once in our mind and second in reality,' Nysha maam stated.

Rajveer looked perplexed and this time I too was trying to understand what she was saying.

"The first part which occurs in our mind is visualization," Nysha maam clarified and she further continued, "Fifth is journaling."

"Wait a minute Nysha Ji. Now everything is going above my head. Can you please hold on?" Rajveer was puzzled and requested her to take a break.

By the time sun had come to their heads and looked yellorangish and was looking good. Hot rays of sun were mixed with cool breeze of garden and it was soothing to body, mind and even soul too.

Both Nysha maam and Rajveer stood up and started walking.

"Relax Rajveer. I'll explain everything to you inch by inch, word by word but don't panic simply by listening some new unknown names," Nysha maam said politely.

"Ok continue," Rajveer said in monotone.

"Journaling means to pen down your thoughts, dreams, desires, your daily routine, likes, dislikes etc," she explained.

Oh journaling meant this thing. I thought it was something related to journalism or something relates to TV or newspaper.

"Sixth is our very own beautiful, GOD gifted nature," she said while raising both her hands to have a look around garden, greenery, trees, flowers, feel of water droplets, sun rays, cool breeze etc.

"And lastly it's mantras," she said.

While Nysha maam was explaining all this, I was counting 1, 2, 3 . . . in my head and finally it stopped; too many techniques to understand.

Rajveer took a deep breathe in and breathe out.

And then one by one Nysha maam explained each and every technique to him.

CHAPTER 6

Positive Thinking

How many times you've come across the people saying to you, "Be Positive"? And how many of you do really know the exact meaning, the exact principle of these 2 words? By saying be positive means you have to avoid negative thoughts and be a possibility thinker. You've to change your moods, thoughts, and actions and most importantly your feelings towards a situation which makes you feel dull, sad, poor, lethargic etc and change your negative feelings into positive one by finding out the best from the worst. Because a change in your thinking will change your situation and that will change the way you see the world.

> *"A pessimist sees the difficulty in every opportunity; an optimist sees the opportunity in every difficulty."*
> —*Winston Churchill*

❧ ❁ ❧

STORY

The only survivor of a shipwreck was washed up on a small, uninhabited island. He prayed feverishly for God to rescue him, and every day he scanned the horizon for help, but none seemed forthcoming.

Exhausted, he eventually managed to build a little hut out of driftwood to protect him from the elements and to store his few possessions. But then one day, after scavenging for food, he arrived home to find his little hut in flames, the smoke rolling up to the sky.

The worst had happened; everything was lost. He was stunned with grief and anger. "God, how could you do this to me!" he cried. Early the next day, however, he was awakened by the sound of a ship that was approaching the island. It had come to rescue him. "How did you know I was here?" asked the weary man of his rescuers. "We saw your smoke signal," they replied.

It is easy to get discouraged when things are going badly. But we shouldn't lose heart, because God is at work in our lives, even in the midst of pain and suffering. Remember, next time your little hut is burning to the ground—it just may be a smoke signal that summons The Grace of God.

❧ ❁ ❧

There are many people who say that they receive what they want. But have you ever given a thought how do they get everything they want. How is it possible that every time they receive, every time their wish is fulfilled, every time their dream is completed? What is the secret behind their story? Are they magicians or God has given them some super natural powers?

I also searched about their secret. Since I was inquisitive to know about it, I got the answer. I come across with the book titled "The Secret" written by "Rhonda Byrne". And when I get through this book believe me; now I also know the secret by a phenomenon called "Law of Attraction" which says that whatever you focus your energy or attention on, you'll attract more of the same. To put it in the simplest terms, "Like attracts like."

Most people don't understand that what they think about, they'll bring about that thing only which means if while driving you fear that you might meet with an accident today, you are sending the message to the universe to create situation that will lead to your accident and if while driving you are happy and moving on with a feeling that you're enjoying while driving and soon you'll reach your destination and start your work, suddenly you'll find that in no time you got the parking and reached your final destination. So it means it all start with your thoughts, words, actions and most importantly your feelings.

The conduit of law of attraction is feelings. So if you're remembering past hurt, anger or frustration; you're attracting more of the same. Just as if you're thinking about what gratitude you have for all the great things in your life—you got it, you're attracting more of the same.

Law of attraction works on three basic principles
1. **Ask** for what you want.
2. **Believe** you can have it.
3. **Receive** when it is offered.

1. **ASK**: For this, firstly clear your mind with all unnecessary thoughts and then focus on what you desire, what do you really want and then ask for it. You don't have to ask over and over either. You just ask once but with the absolute belief that you'll receive it. There is an old African saying that goes, "When you pray, move your feet." Asking means; moving forward with the intention to receive. Asking means taking necessary steps required towards achieving your goal and as law of attraction says; like attracts like and the universe will reward you by giving what you want.

2. **Believe**: After asking for your dream, believe in it and live as if your dream has already been fulfilled. Act as if you have already achieved your goal or start thinking and living from the perspective of "thinking from the end" which says that you've got what you want and now you're very happy and enjoying the very moment you desired of. Say for example you want to have your own well furnished new home. Start seeing yourself already living in that home. Focus your mind over that home and put your thoughts over

color of walls, furniture you want in your house, curtains, cutlery in kitchen. Picture all these stuff in your mind and start feeling happy to have such a lovely home. Always remember, that you are seeking is also seeking you.

3. **Receive**: This step is very easy. You have to do nothing over it except than to receive it with your open heart and get that feeling of happiness. When you focus your mind on your desires and believe in yourself by visualizing what you want is yours now, the universe will give you your gift.

So it all starts with your positive thoughts. Positive thinking is the foundation of the law of attraction. Build your foundation strong. A house starts with a foundation and not with roof. Make your foundation strong by being happy and living healthy and successful life and tell yourself that you can do it and there is no such thing that you can't achieve. So what exactly is positive thinking? It is like that echo point where you hear the same words what you speak. The same can be said for what you think. What goes in your mind has the power to shape what you think, what you believe and ultimately how you behave. As Mahatma Gandhi has very well said, "A man is the product of his thoughts, what he thinks, he becomes."

Story: Positive Thinking

Once upon a time there was a businessman who went to another city for some office work. On his way there was a dense forest. It was a sunny day and he was moving through the forest for whole day. He becomes tired so he sat under a tree and took rest. It was not an ordinary tree. It was wish tree. Specialty of this wish tree was that whosoever will sit under its shadow and asks for any wish or desire will be fulfilled immediately. The businessman felt relaxed under that tree. Now he was feeling thirsty and wished if he could get some cold water to drink. That's it!! At that very moment wish tree had fulfilled the businessman's desire. A pot full of cold water was in front of him and he quenched his thirst. After sometime he felt hungry and thinking in his mind if he could get some food to eat and he got it. Now he was feeling sleepy and desired of a bed and again he got it.

Now that his hunger and thirst are over and he got a bed to sleep, he was thinking—"I'm feeling very sleepy but how can I sleep? This is such dense forest and what if a lion comes and kills me?" Now this man had brought negative thoughts in his mind and the wish tree has also fulfilled this. The man didn't think that if his positive thoughts are fulfilled, the same can be done with negative thoughts.

So what we learn from this story is always think positive. Our universe is like that wish tree that is waiting for our command to fulfill. So we'll get what we'll give. Be aware of what you're thinking because this universe works on our thoughts.

> *"A person who has good thoughts cannot ever be ugly. You can have a wonky nose and a crooked mouth and a double chin and stick out teeth, but if you have good thoughts they will shine out of your face like sunbeams and you will always look lovely."*
> —*Roald Dahl*

It is rather to feel positive when everything goes well but when circumstances goes worse, every normal human being's mind will focus only negative thoughts. When people face problems, they indulge in wrong activities, feel bad and helpless, become resentful and angry and start fearing from all the problems. Does this attitude help you in anything? No, it will only get you deeper into problems, because what you seek is also seeking you and thus you create more problems.

Wherever you're now, whatever your situation is, there is always a way out. This might require a different way of thinking, a different approach or developing a new skill. Forget the past as you cannot change it, but you can change your present and when you can change your present, you can also change your future. Like any other, being positive skill requires gradual development and training. No one can speak foreign language in one day. In life, there will be enough times when you'll feel depressed. Disappointed and annoyed. But you don't have to really look over them. You have a wonderful world around which is so beautiful, you have your own family, your best friends to support you in every situation then why to focus your mind on negative situations.

This can be read as "GOD IS NO WHERE" or as "GOD IS NOW HERE"; everything depends on how you see it. So think positive always.

> *"If you don't like something change it, if you can't change it, change the way you think about it."*
>
> *—Mary Engelbreit*

Practical instructions to develop positive thinking

1. Try to find out positive in every situation, in every person and in your daily routine life.

> *"Everyday may not be good, but there is something good in every day."*
>
> *—Unknown*

❧ ✄ ☙

STORY

A lady went to a Psychiatrist. She told the Doctor that she is going to leave a company because the Boss was not approachable and always blame, accuse and ill-treat her. Then, the Doctor advised her if she could follow what he tells. A lady told her definitely she could do that. Then, the Doctor advised her to pick up a good thing from her boss, say if he dressed well, she could say your shirt is very nice and something similar daily for three months and then come to the doctor. If she still wants to leave the company, then she could leave. The Lady told the doctor how she could do this if the boss is totally a person who has no good habit or any good things to say. The Doctor said you will be having lot of moments with him in a day. Find one of them for the whole day and say that to him. With hesitation the lady told the doctor she would do that.

After 3 months, the lady came to the doctor and the doctor asked her what happened. She told him she is going to leave the company. The Doctor asked if the Boss still behaves like what the lady told earlier. The Lady told she is going to get married, so she is leaving the company. The Doctor asked what about the boss. The Lady told the doctor he is her fiancé. The Life has changed for her. What really happened, if anyone knows?

❧ ✄ ☙

This is what we think, speak and do which have a drastic result in our life.

2. Always use only positive words while thinking and talking. Use words such as "I can", "I am

able", "I am the best", "It is possible" and "It can be done." Etc

3. Allow into your awareness only feelings of happiness, strength and success.

4. Ignore negative thoughts and substitute negative thought with a positive one. It is as if there are two pictures in front of you, and you choose to look at one of them and disregard the other.

5. Before desiring for something, visualize its picture in your mind and its successful outcome and then start working towards it as if you've already received it.

6. Read at least one page of inspiring book everyday.

7. Watch movies that make you feel happy.

8. Read autobiographies of great successful people.

9. Associate yourself with the people who are positive thinkers.

10. Always sit and walk with your back straight. This will strengthen your confidence and inner strength.

11. Engage yourself in any such activity which fills you full of joy and energy like playing basketball, dancing, swimming, and running,

playing with a kid or anything you like. This will allow positive energy to flow within your body and mind.

12. Make a list of positive things you have in your life and daily look that paper and thank God that there are so many things you have to be happy.

STORY

A man once telephoned Norman Vincent Peale. He was despondent and told the reverend that he had nothing left to live for. Norman Vincent Peale invited the man over to his office. "Everything is gone, hopeless," the man told him. "I'm living in deepest darkness. In fact, I've lost heart for living altogether."

Norman Vincent Peale smiled sympathetically.

"Let's take a look at your situation," he said calmly. On a sheet of paper he drew a vertical line down the middle. He suggested that they list on the left side the things the man had lost, and on the right, the things he had left. "You won't need that column on the right side," said the man sadly. "I have nothing left, period."

Norman Vincent Peale asked, "When did your wife leave you?"

"What do you mean? She hasn't left me. My wife loves me!"

"That's great!" said Norman Vincent Peale enthusiastically. "Then that will be number one in the right-hand column—Wife hasn't left. Now, when were your children jailed?"

"That's silly. My children aren't in jail!"

"Good! That's number two in the right-hand column—Children not in jail," said Norman Vincent Peale, jotting it down.

After a few more questions in the same vein, the man finally got the point and smiled in spite of himself. "Funny, how things change when you think of them that way," he said.

13. Try doing all these exercises daily (again and again) until it becomes your habit.

At last I would like to conclude by saying that life is like the ocean; sometimes rough sometimes calm; full of ups and downs. Certain situations come in life when you feel disappointed and defeated. It is the positive thinking that helps you come out of the frustrating situation. The fact is that whether you think positively or negatively, you shape your life accordingly. Negative thoughts can divert your attention from your plans. And thinking positively can change your entire life. It is a key to success in every aspect of life. So positive and negative are directions, which direction do you choose???

CHAPTER 7

Practical Techniques

L istening to someone's talk is very easy but to apply them in our daily routine life becomes quite ignorable. You must have seen there is a line written on every cigarette packet, "Smoking is injurious to health." People, who smoke already knows that smoking will affect their life and body functioning still they become ignorant of what they see, read or listen about the harmful effects of smoking. Similarly as in the case of Yog Guru Ramdev Baba who repeatedly says that by doing yoga your body will be relaxed and you'll feel yourself into a completely new world. What do you think if 1000 people are listening to him, how many would have really tried to do yoga? There are many people who follow him but still there are people who even after listening pays no attention of how useful it can be for someone.

So basically the problem does not lie with the cigarette packet or Yog Guru Ramdev Baba, the problem is within ourselves. We ask for all the things of what to do but we do not implement them in our life. As I said asking and listening is very easy but what one need to do is implement. Don't just see, have the vision; don't just read, understand; don't just touch, feel it; don't just live the life, love it. And when people don't do anything they give excuses like, "I don't know how to do it", "It can't be done by me", "I'm not capable."

People always complain about bad things happening in their life. They often say, "Our income is very low, my body doesn't support me, I'm very ill, why all the bad stuff happens with me, I'm fed up with all the stress." But do these people have really taken any initiative to resolve their problem, to find out any alternative way to get back to normal life? Your life has given solution to all your problems, its just that you have to find it. People often know what do they want but most of them don't know how it can be achieved. Even if you don't know the HOW part, you need not to worry, here are some of the practical techniques that you can apply in your life to reduce stress and live a joyful life. We just have to change our outlook towards our problems. So whenever you're not feeling good or your mood is off, try to do some of the following techniques and repeat it on a regular basis and then I guarantee you that you'll definitely feel the difference and will live in your own comfort zone, fully relaxed.

1. Positive Affirmations

Affirmations are positive statements that describe a desired situation which are repeated many times in order to impress the subconscious mind and trigger it into positive action. To ensure the effectiveness of the affirmations, it has to be repeated with firm conviction, faith, attention, desire, and interest and with feelings. The repeated words help you focus your mind on your aim and automatically build corresponding mental images in the conscious mind which will affect the subconscious mind. These repeated words are merely methods to convince your subconscious mind and to activate it and make it work on what you want. So whenever you want to do something, you first have to say it to yourself. And when you'll be aware of what you say, you'll have control over your thoughts which in turn will control your mind and your life.

> *"Affirmations are like seed planted in soil. Poor soil, poor growth, rich soil, abundant growth. The more you choose to think thoughts that make you feel good, the quicker the affirmations work."*
> —*Louise L. Hay*

Positive affirmations can release you from the chairs of negative thinking that may have been sabotaging your attempts to live a happier and healthier life. How successful and happy we are, is often defined not by what happens to us but rather how we react to the events in our lives. Poor self esteem and negative thoughts force us to belief that what is happening to us is because of our own destiny. Change this thought. You are the creator of your destiny and you can live your life the way you want by simply repeating positive affirmations relating to your needs and desire. As Napolean Hill says, "Whatever the mind of man can conceive and believe; it can achieve." So our first target is our mind to which we have to take control of.

Your mind is like a sponge which soaks all the information given to it by the surrounding. So you have to be aware of what you are feeding to your mind. If you feed positive, your mind will react positively and vice-versa. The whole purpose of using affirmations is to convince your mind that you're consistently affirming is the truth and that convincing factor is emotions. Emotion is the driving force that powers your affirmations. Your subconscious mind will not be able to turn your affirmations into reality unless you attach a high emotional energy to every statement. Your subconscious mind responds best when emotion is present. So create the life you've always dreamt of through the power of affirmations.

You must have heard the story of Pavlov's dog. Ivan Pavlon, a Russian physiologist was doing a research on digestive process of dog. And while doing his research he got to know some other unexpected results. In the research, the dog was provided to listen the sound of a bell and then given a piece of meat after which the dog started salvation. The same thing was done for nest consecutive days and dogs starts secreting saliva. But one day Pavlon only ringed the bell and to his notice dog starting salving in the absence of meat. It means the neutral stimulus (sound of bell) with another unconditional stimulus (smell of meat) results in unconditioned response (Salvation).

So the story reveals the fundamental of how unusual things can be done. When bell was ringing and food was presented, it entered in the subconscious mind of the dog that whenever the bell will ring, food is presented and so he started salivating. Since the process was repeated again and again, one fine day when only bell rang, salivation occurs. Now just refer this experiment to your own life. When a neutral stimulus (positive affirmations) along with unconditioned stimulus (desire, faith, commitment to reach your goal) is continuously fed into your subconscious mind, it will result into an unconditioned response (Your achievements).

And also remember one thing while repeating positive affirmations; feel it as if it had already happened. If you feel positive for that moment and again started bringing negative thoughts rest of the day, it won't work. You have to refuse negative thinking and repeat positive affirmations in present tense. Like if you want to be rich then don't say I'll be rich which says that you'll be rich in indefinite future which nobody knows, instead say this, "I'm rich now" and the subconscious mind will work over it all the time and make this happen now in this very moment.

> *"As long as you know what it is you desire,*
> *then by simply affirming at it is yours*
> *firmly and positively, with no ifs and buts,*
> *or maybes over and over again, from the*
> *minute you arise in the morning until the*
> *time you go to sleep at night, and as many*
> *times during the day as your work and*
> *activities permit, you will be drawn to those*

> ***people, places and events that will bring your desires to you."***
> **—Scott Reed**

Affirmations will not only make you feel better about yourself and your life but if used correctly, they can manifest real change in your life. There are many ways to say affirmations like you can affirm in front of mirror, you can write affirmations on paper and read it daily or you can even sing the affirmations. Whatever way you choose, the basic fundamental of using them is feelings. Feel them with full passion and affirm them daily and get it fitted into your subconscious mind.

Here are some of the affirmations related to job, life, health, relationships, harmony, abundance, self esteem, and peace, security which you can speak daily and you can also alter them according to your need.

- My body heals quickly and easily.
- I give out love and it is returned to me multiplied.
- I have a wonderful partner and we both are happy and at peace.
- I attract only healthy relationships.
- I am unique.
- I am safe.
- I am at peace.
- I trust myself.
- I love the way I am.
- I rejoice in whatever I do.
- My income is constantly increasing.
- I have unlimited potential to complete any task.
- My life is filled with joy and love.

- I am willing to forgive.
- I have a lot of energy.
- My thoughts are under my control.
- I have the perfect job for me.
- My mind is calm.
- I am living in the house of my dreams.
- I have a wonderful and satisfying job.
- I am successful at whatever I do.
- I have the means to travel anywhere I want.
- Everything is getting better everyday.
- My future is glorious.
- All my dreams have come true.

2. Meditation

Is there any single moment in your daily schedule of 24 hours wherein your mind was completely free and was not wandered by any single thought? Is there any work you do with full attention and concentration? Has it ever happened with you that you're working on one project still your mind is thinking something else after every few minutes? Has it ever happened with you that you're driving to reach certain destination and actually you drove to some other place?

I'm sure you all must have faced one or the other thing asked an above paragraph. Have you ever given a thought why all these things happen? Why our mind is always surrounded by hundred of thoughts? Why can't we focus on one particular thing? It's all because now-a-days we have involved ourselves in the outer world so much that we cannot reconnect to our inner world. All other stuff is more important to us rather than from ourselves. We are more attracted towards fashion, disco, studies, promotion, salary hike, break ups, movies, pornography etc that we have in reality forgotten ourselves as is "Who we are?" and "Why we are here?"

Because of so much involvement in the outer world we become tired, sometimes stressful, feel resented, uncomfortable or may be at times out of the world. As a result we indulge ourselves in bad habits like drinking, smoking and drug addiction and become disrespectful, irresponsible, double dealer and start gaining the feeling of envy, jealousy, hatred and greed.

Just take a moment and think, "we are here to celebrate the pain or we are here to enjoy the life given to us." Life is like a school and we draw to ourselves the events, circumstances and relationships we need to help us grow. Every problem comes with 2 choices to expand or to contract our consciousness. Do we become defensive and self protective? Or do we see challenges as opportunities to become stronger, to learn and to expand. If we contract our hearts and mind we'll experience pain which will result in stressful life. On the contrary, if we relax our heart and mind, we'll fill ourselves with happiness, joy and fulfillment.

So the way to relax our mind is Meditation. It is the art of being aware and conscious in our day to day living. Any action done with awareness is meditation. It means to be fully aware of our actions, thoughts, feelings and emotions. A meditative person is fully conscious in one's action. It is the art of staying in this present moment.

A sleeping person either lives in the past moment or is dreaming about the future life. But a meditator stays in this present moment ad is alert about his thoughts and actions. Like when we are eating food; our total attention should be on eating rather than watching TV, talking over phone, planning for tomorrow's meeting or just looking outside the home. Our mind is a very good runner as it runs behind every materialistic thing and through meditation we can catch our mind and get it relaxed and focus it onto what we want.

> *"Meditation is not a way of making your mind quite. It's a way of entering into the quite that's already there—buried under the 50000 thoughts the average person thinks every day."*
>
> **—Deepak Chopra**

❧ ✳ ❧

STORY: Budha and His Disciple

Once Buddha was walking from one town to another with few of his followers. This was in the initial days. While they were traveling, they happened to pass a lake. They stopped there and Buddha told one of his disciples, "I am thirsty. Do get me some water from that lake there."

The disciple walked up to the lake. When he reached it, he noticed that some people were washing clothes in the water and, right at that moment, a bullock cart started crossing through the lake. As a result, the water became very muddy, very turbid. The disciple thought, "How can I give this muddy water to Buddha to drink!" So he came back and told Buddha, "The water in there is very muddy. I don't think it is fit to drink."

After about half an hour, again Buddha asked the same disciple to go back to the lake and get him some water to drink. The disciple obediently went back to the lake. This time he found that the lake had absolutely clear water in it. The mud had settled down and the water above it looked fit to be had. So he collected some water in a pot and brought it to Buddha.

Buddha looked at the water, and then he looked up at the disciple and said, "See what you did to make the water clean. You let it be . . . and the mud settled down on its own—and you got clear water . . . Your mind is also like that. When it is disturbed, just let it be. Give it a little time. It will settle down on its own. You don't have to put in any effort to calm it down. It will happen. It is effortless."

What did Buddha emphasize here? He said, "It is effortless." Having 'peace of mind' is not a strenuous job; it is an effortless process. When there is peace inside you, that peace permeates to the outside. It spreads around you and in the environment, such that people around you start feeling that peace and grace stressful life.

So the effortless process over here is meditation. Whatever your mind is doing let it be and focus yourself onto one point, one thought, one statement and then flow all your energy onto that one single point.

> *"Meditation is sticking to one thought. That single thought keeps away other thoughts, distraction of mind is a sign of its weakness; by constant meditation it gains strength."*
> —*Sri Ramana Maharshi*

How to do it?

To start up with meditation firstly find out a clean place to sit. Then sit in a position which is most comfortable to you; either you sit cross legged or you can also sit on a chair with your foot touching the ground. Now close your eyes and just relax, let go your thoughts and do nothing. Let your thoughts quite down. Gradually focus your attention on the darkness behind your eye lids. Be conscious to that one single point and pay attention to it. Try to be detached, if any thought is entering in your mind; don't react, don't give any judgment, simply observe it and let it go. To increase your concentration you can chant any mantra or prayer or you can repeat any God's name or you can also focus on your breathing pattern (deep and regular). Meditate like this for 10 minutes in your early days and time limit can be increased as day passes and then open your eyes slowly.

Initially you'll find it tough or boring but as you practice it regularly; you'll experience relaxation, increased awareness, mental focus, clarity and a sense of peace in your mind. It is a powerful tool. It calms you and connects you to the source, clears your mind and leaves you more centered. It helps you make better decisions, become healthier, change bad habits and negative thought pattern.

> *"Prayer is when you talk to God; meditation is when you listen to God."*
> *—Diana Robinson*

Benefits of Meditation

- Worries and struggles of the mind are smoothened.
- Fear is removed.
- Sense of joy penetrates in your daily life.
- You'll be filled with sense of peace and love.
- You attain a sense of fulfillment and perfection.
- You'll come to know about the within, the real YOU.
- Leads to a deeper level of physical relaxation.
- Enhance immune system.
- Enhance energy and strength.
- Builds self confidence.
- Helps to control your thoughts.
- Increase creativity.
- Improved learning ability and memory.
- Purifies your character.
- Changes attitude towards life.

- Helps living in the present moment.
- Brings body, mind and spirit in harmony.
- Reduces stress.

3. Visualization

What is Visualization?

Visualization is the intentional process of creating a mental image, feeling or sense perception of something you want. Actually, we all do this all the time without even realizing it. Anytime when you make plans for future like planning for vacation, mental images goes on in your mind about your vacation; as if what you'll wear, where to stay, what fun you'll be doing etc; it means you're visualizing. And often most people use this visualization technique for negative things rather than for positive ones.

Why it is necessary?

To understand this lets look at our brain. Our brain is divided in 2 parts; left and right. Left brain is responsible for logical reasoning and right brain for creativity. In our daily routine life, we focus more on our left brain to perform all our daily activities and very few people uses right portion of brain. This causes an imbalance in the brain; so by yielding to our right brain we access a balanced connection between two sides of brain and even opens up for a change and renewal. And visualization is all about creative imagination. One can be so creative in imagining the things like in fantasy books and in kids world where fairies, Mickey Mouse, Donald duck, superman etc can be created so the same imagination can be used in our life to live it the way we want and attract all the things we desire for. So scientifically visualization is necessary to balance our brain and psychologically it is necessary to achieve what we want to live life the king's size.

3 W's
Who, When & Where

Visualization is imagination and imagination is creativity. So anyone and everyone is capable enough to imagine and create his own world. This technique is not only restricted for riches and not only necessary for poor. It can be done by every person of any age who desires to be what he wants. Also it can be done anytime whether traveling or sitting, during day or night, sitting alone or in a group. The moment you start visualizing is the moment it can be done. And creativity and imagination needs no specific place to work upon; what it requires is the thoughts, feelings and actions to convert it into a reality.

How Does It Work?

Dream / Desire → Emotions & Feelings → Physical Sensation / Reality / Action

This is very well explained by an example. When you watch a horror movie, you start creating images about it, you start thinking about that scary person in the movie, create a mental picture in your mind about the character and his actions (thoughts and images) and you get frightened and nervous (emotions and feelings) and ultimately you get goose bumps (a physical sensation). So it means visualization provides images for the mind that change your emotions that generate a feeling which turns into a sensation. That's how it works.

> *"Visualize the thing you want, see it, feel it, and believe in it. Make your mental blue print and begin to build."*
> —**Robert Collier**

Your Mind is your Jinee

You might have heard about the story of Alladin and his Jinee wherein whatever Alladin says to Jinee; he does it. So here you're the Alladin and your mind is Jinee who will perform all the actions whatever you say whatever you want. Your Jinee will take you to the place where you wish to be, place all the delicious dishes you want to eat and give you all the desired money you wish for.

In order to keep control of your Jinee and make it work and fulfill all your desires; all you have to do is dream your dreams, think your thoughts and speak the words that are in resonance with your desires and get the feelings. You can do this in your day to day, moment to moment situations of your life. Repeat this process and apply it on every small or big dream, any short term or long term goal of your life and get the results. As you're most repeated thoughts will not only dominate your mental world; but your material world too. The stronger are the feelings and emotions that are associated with your thoughts and mental images, the stronger is their impact on your life.

So always pay attention to the thoughts and images that passes through your mind. Find out what sort of thoughts often come in your mind? Are these thoughts constructive or destructive; positive or negative? Gives you happiness or sadness? Do you feel excited or depressed? Control your thoughts and imagination and so will control your mind.

> *"Ordinary people believe only in the possible. Extra ordinary people visualize not what is possible or probable, but rather what is impossible. And by visualizing the impossible, they begin to see it as possible."*
> —*Cherie Carter Scott*

> *"I've discovered that numerous peak performers use the skill of mental rehearsal of visualization. They mentally run through important events before they happen."*
> —*Charles A. Garfield*

STORY

Once upon a time there were 3 sportsperson who were practicing for their final game. First one was focusing on practice, practice and only practice. He tried all his level best to perform whole day and night. Second one was a bit different. He divides his 80% of his time for practice and remaining 20% time for visualization sessions. Third one did nothing except visualizing. His total spotlight was on visualization. And do you know who won the game? Yes, the third sportsperson. This is the magic of visualization. It really works.

4. Journaling

> **"The positive thing about writing is that you connect with yourself in the deepest way, and that's heaven. You get a chance to know who you are, to know what you think. You begin to have relationship with your mind."**
>
> **—Natalie Goldberg**

Journaling is simply the process of regularly writing your thoughts down on the paper. Everybody's life is full of ups and downs and nobody would like to remember his past bad experiences. If a person is sitting alone and smiling; it means he is memorizing some of his past good experiences, time spend with someone so special or reminding the special moment he'd gone through which ultimately brought smile on his face. So journaling is basically writing down your thoughts, feelings and emotions on a notebook so that you can connect to yourself anytime you want. Each person has his or her unique life where they experience different lessons of life to learn from. So if you think that your life is a journey then your journal will become different stations which will come along to reach your destination. It's all about sharing your views about every station and the feelings you recall in your mind while traveling through the journey of life. The journal becomes your map of self discovery. In this fast moving modern life, it gives you an opportunity to stop and reflect upon the events, circumstances and people coming in your life.

The process of journaling will enable you to understand who you are? What do you feel about certain situation or person? How do you react to a situation? What are you passionate about? What are you afraid of? What is it that you can't live without? What you were earlier and what you are now? Is there nay personal change? Is there any spiritual change? What is your behavioral attitude etc? Your journal is like your personal diary wherein you would record the things that were significant to you, you might write down about your feelings and reaction toward a particular person/event, you can write about what excites you, what is bothering you or you might also write down a list of good things happen in a day.

Keeping a journal is one of the most important tools towards developing your life because it forces you to get sometime for yourself and to ponder upon your thoughts, feelings, emotions, likes and dislikes, dreams etc to clarify them and to organize them in such manner that it results in profound changes the way you think and act upon it.

And I must say I myself have been so influenced by this that now I also had a habit of writing my own personal journal. I write about important events of my life, my feelings towards a person, about what I want to be, my friends, my family, my inspiration, my goals. Everything which I say to myself when I'm alone is written in my journal. It is the easiest type of writing because it doesn't involve anyone but you. You're the only reader. So you don't have to worry about grammar, punctuation, logic and content. Whenever you feel like writing, just take a pen and your journal and start writing. Don't phrase sentences in your mind, just write and eventually you'll find the words of your feelings you wanted to write. You can write whatever comes in your mind without any hesitation because it's all about you and your feelings. It is not being written for others, so mechanics is not an issue. It is just a way to express oneself in a creative way which is a good way to release feelings that you might otherwise hide or suppress. It is the ultimate self help tool and also the most cost efficient.

5. Exercise

> *"Those who think they have not time for bodily exercise will sooner or later have to find time for illness."*
> —*Edward Stanley*

Before starting or saying anything I would just like to ask you some questions and you just have to reply in Yes or No.

1. Do you keep your skin clean?
2. Do you brush your teeth?
3. Do you comb your hair?
4. Do you go out well dressed?
5. Do you eat two times a day?
6. Do you use your mobile daily?
7. Do you have time to watch TV?
8. Do you plan your vacations?
9. Do you chat with your friends?

After reading all these questions you must be thinking why I'm asking you such silly and simple questions. I know these questions are silly but I just wanted to know what your answers were. I'm sure you've got a "Yes" to most of the questions. Am I right? It's because most of the people do perform all these tasks in their daily routine life. I know there is no wonder in asking such questions. But now I want to ask you one more question. Do You Exercise Regularly?

Some of you might say "Yes" but most of the people don't pay attention to the word "Exercise." According to some people, exercise is such an activity only for those who are free, who don't have anything else to do. But actually now-a-days, it is the most crucial part of our life where everybody should do it. Those who are not doing it are missing out an important part of the healthier lifestyle. No matter what your age or shape is; you should exercise daily. Not only does exercise tone your body so you can wear your favourite jeans but also does lot more than this. Let us look at some of the incredible benefits of exercise then talk about how you can get start with it.

> *"A man's health can be judged by which he take two at a time, pills or stairs."*
> *—Joan Welsh*

Benefits of Exercise

1. Strengthen your muscle.
2. Keeps your bones strong.
3. Improves your skin.
4. Increased relaxation.
5. Strong immune system.
6. Controls weight.
7. Improves your mood.
8. Boosts your energy.
9. Promotes better sleep.
10. Enhance work, recreation and sport performance.
11. Reduce the risk of heart attack.
12. Reduce high blood pressure.
13. Reduce cholesterol.
14. Reduce the risk of cancer.
15. Reduce the risk of developing diabetes.

16. Reduce depression and anxiety.
17. Puts the spark back into your sex life.
18. Exercise can be fun.

Now that we've come across the benefits of exercise, we must know the holistic view of exercise. Most of the people know only about physical exercise but there is lot more than this. We will be coming to it in further pages but first let know about the fundamentals of physical exercise.

1. Physical Exercise

Human body is designed to walk, run, jump and dance. Basically we are made to move. But unfortunately we spend most of our time in watching TV, sitting in front of our PC and laptops or enjoy sleeping. Do all these activities pay something in return to us? Are these really necessary to live our livelihood or to survive? You have your answer. Just give a thought that there are 1440 minutes and now analyze how do you spend this; going to school, office, sleep, study, party, chatting on mobile, watching TV etc. To stay healthy, fit and fine and enjoy a happier life just schedule your 30 minutes for physical activity.

Regular exercise is a critical part of staying healthy. People, who are active, live longer and feel better. Don't confuse your mind of understanding exercise as a vigorous work out or going to the gym and sweating a lot. There are a lot many other ways to do exercise which include walking briskly, mowing the lawn, dancing, swimming, bicycling, stretching etc. There are many ways of doing exercise but what is more important is that you do it. There are only two requirements when it comes to exercise. One is that you do it; the other is that you continue to do it. The key is to find the right exercise for you. It is fun and you stay more likely to stay motivated. Exercise not only makes you physically fitter, it also improves your mental health and general sense of well being.

> *"The only valid excuse for not exercising is paralysis."*
> —*Moira Nardholt*

2. Mental Exercise

A machine stops working when it stays in passive mode for a longer duration of time. Similarly, if our brain stops working our body will stop functioning and will not perform its daily routine activities. In order to get work done from our machine (our brain) we have to nurture it by applying some basic regular exercises which will indulge our brain to be in active mode and work properly. One just has to use his/her mind in some activities. Don't sit idle and don't waste your precious time. You can utilize it by doing mental exercise to keep your brain in perfect moving mode. Some of these exercises include doing crossword puzzles, playing chess, attempting to memorize a grocery list before you go to the store; stimulation of brain can occur in variety of ways.

A simple way to activate your brain is to doing the things in opposite manner like using non dominant hand for eating, brushing the teeth, dialing the phone etc. Incorporating as many of the five senses as possible into everyday activities can stimulate the brain. It is important to challenge your brain to learn new and novel tasks, especially processes that you've never done before. Other activities include using your one or two of the 5 senses in your daily routine life like get dressed with your eyes closed, wash your hair with closed eyes, listen to music, smell flowers and identify them etc. Thus, our brain is a thinking organ that learns and grows by interacting with the world through perception and action. Mental stimulation improves brain function.

3. Spiritual Exercise

Spiritual exercise connects yourself to your inner world just as your eyes connect you to your outer world. Spiritual exercise include meditation, yoga, positive affirmation etc which are already discussed previously.

6. Nature, Music and Mantra

Whenever people are in stress I use to analyze them. I've my friends, colleagues, my family members and relatives who at times feel depressed or undergo stress and tensions due to one or other reasons life gives to them. I use to ask them, "What do you want to do now at this particular moment? What is that one good feeling which if given to you will change your mood and you'll feel refreshing?" And most of them answers like this, "I want to go in nature's lap.", "I wish I could be in quite place in between several trees and grass", "I wish I could fly between these clouds.", "I wish right now I would have been in Kashmir (earth's heaven)."

Spending time in nature makes people more alive. Several studies have been done showing that interaction with nature bring energizing effects both physically and mentally. Whenever people arein stressful environments like hospitals, remote military sites or feeling homesickness; it is the healing effect of nature which relieves from stress and improves well being. Nature is the fuel for soul. Often when we feel depleted, we reach for a cup of coffee, but what I suggest is a better way to get energized is connect with nature.

> *"I go to nature to be soothed and healed, and to have my senses put in order."*
> —*John Burroughs*

> *"We need to find God and he cannot be found in noise and restlessness. God is the friend of silence. See how nature— trees, flowers, grass grows in silence; see the starts, the sun and the moon, how they move in silence. We need silence to be able to touch souls."*
> —*Mother Teresa*

So the best remedy for those who feel afraid, lonely or unhappy is to go outside, watch the nature, connect yourself to it, forget all your past bad memories and appreciate nature's beauty. Watch the moving clouds, dance in the rain, get the feel of the wind, smell the mud of rainy season, see how birds fly, how these flowers get their different shapes and colors. By seeing nature and enjoying it, you'll forget what you were thinking the very last moment. It's the best way to connect yourself with your soul.

Music

> *"Music is the mediator between the spiritual and sensual life."*
> —*Beethoven*

All of us like listening to music and each one of us has an individualistic preferences. We at times listens song in a car or sing melody song while walking, we may have listened music at wedding party or in our college fare well party. Even though tastes differ, but each one of us listens to music and has a favorite singer or band and I bet every one of us taps our feet while listening to music.

Music is not only fun but gratifying. Music touches our soul. We'll find music everywhere let it be dentist clinic, truck, a hyper market, a grocery shop, or even where cricket and basket ball players practice. Music gives us soothing effect and reduces stress. It makes people feel good. Many experts suggest that music is an incredible tool for stress management. Music can help keep us in a relaxed state during periods of high stress or even help us get to sleep. Music therapy can help reduce the strife caused by stress, physical or mental pain, anxiety or panic attacks, anger, attitude and mood changes and difficulty with sleeping.

> *"Take a music bath once or twice a week*
> *for a few seasons. You will find it is to the*
> *soul what a water bath is to the body."*
> *—Oliver Wendell Holmes*

Music seems to be part of our biological heritage. Mother's everywhere sing to their infants because babies understand it. This is the reason why music has a comforting effect on us because it reminds us of the first time we heard it in our mother's womb. Music can do lots of wonders in our life. Music can tell story of our life in 3 minutes, music can change our mood, music can make us remind of a past good moment, music can bring our near and dear ones to us, music is the medium to express our feelings, music can bring tears in our eyes, music can make you fall in love or may remind you to the time when your heart was broken.

As Berthhold Aurebach states, "Music washes away from the soul the dust of everyday life." The best way to de stress yourself is to listen your favorite music. This will ease your heartbeat and relax you. And to people who loves to be with nature are provided with nature's sound wherein they can hear music of the birds, the wind and the rustling leaves. You can also found these sounds of woods or the oceans or waterfall captured in a CD.

Benefits from Music

- Reduces the feeling of fatigue.
- Give the patient a sense of control.
- Increase in level of psychological arousal.
- Physiological relaxation response.

- Improvement in motor co-ordination.
- Causes body to release endorphins to counteract pain.
- Serves as a distracter.
- Helps to work more productively.
- Calms, relaxes and helps to sleep.
- Improves mood and decreases depression.

Chants / Mantra

"Mananaat traavate iti mantrals"
That which uplifts by constant repetition is Mantra.

In this chapter we had discussed many of the practical techniques to remove stress. At last we had discussed about the importance and effect of music on our body. As the soft sound of wind rusting through leaves soothes our nerves, the musical note of running stream enchants our heart, thunders may cause awe of fear; in the same way chanting any mantra connects us to the inner self. Sound of mantra can lift the believer towards the higher self. Everybody knows that the good health requires proper diet, adequate exercise and sufficient rest. Similarly for our spiritual nourishment we need to reach our soul and the way to connect to our soul is to meditate and chant the mantras.

This mantra does vary accordingly like Gayatri Mantra, humming note of OM, Shiva mantra and many more. Each mantra has its own advantages. As one develops more realization by chanting, he perceives the original spiritual existence of the self. According to Bhagvad Gita, this enlightened state is characterized by one's ability to see the self by pure mind and to rejoice in the self. By chanting one can control his mind. And the one who had conquered his mind, then his mind is the best of friends.

I myself practice it in my daily routine life. I'd make a habit of repeating Gayatri mantra in my morning sessions and as a result now I feel relaxed, motivated, elevated and most importantly happy. Every time I get depressed or get angry with someone, I use to take control of my mind and stat chanting Gayatri mantra; slowly and gradually my anger goes down and I become normal. Now this has become my spiritual health requirement and if we ignore it, we will be suppressed by material tendencies like anxiety, hatred, loneliness, prejudice, greed, boredom, envy and anger.

So in order to counteract these infections we have to take regular medicines and vaccines of mantra's as described in our Vedic literature to get spiritual strength, steady inner growth and clarity of thought. When we indulge ourselves in material possessions, eventually we loose awareness of our real spiritual self and start encountering all sort of fear like fear of loosing someone, fear of death, fear of old age, fear of becoming ill. But by chanting, we realize ourselves to be pure and completely distinct from our material body. Because the mantra is a completely pure spiritual sound vibration, it has power to restore our consciousness to its original uncontaminated condition. Chanting gives inner satisfaction as it places us in direct contact with the inner self.

6th Meeting

8 . . . . 9 . . . . 10 . . . . 11 . . . .

Speed of trade mill was increasing after every 2 minutes and Rajveer in his shorts and sandoz wearing adidas shoes was running on it. He has his headsets on his ears and was enjoying the music too.

He was all wet with his sweat but still he continued running.

After few moments Nysha maam came in and was looking for Rajveer. This was Talwalkar's gym where Rajveer had called Nysha maam for their next meeting. It was 6:00 pm in the evening.

Nysha maam was looking here and there and was searching Rajveer and finally she found him.

"Hi Rajveer," Nysha maam greeted.

"Oh hello Nysha Ji," Rajveer said while removing his headset and immediately looked above to see the time in watch placed on the wall and said, "Wow! You're exactly on time."

"Rajveer, I usually use to come on time but I wonder how come today you're before time?" Nysha maam asked shockingly.

Rajveer continued on trade mill and Nysha maam was standing beside.

"Well Nysha Ji, in our last meeting you said something about exercise right?" Rajveer asked.

"Yes."

"And I'd already told you how much I love my body and earlier I use to do exercise a lot."

"Yes, you'd shared it with me," Nysha maam nodded.

"So I'm listening to you, implementing on what you've suggested me and doing my best to improve myself and come out of this crowd," Rajveer said.

"I'm impressed Rajveer," she said.

Rajveer stopped the trade mill, step down aside and paused to take breathe. He was falling short of breath.

Both of them moved towards pec deck machine. A machine over which one can sit, expand the arms and pull the bars in front of the chest; basically done for shoulders, back and chest.

Rajveer moved towards this machine and started working out and Nysha maam sat on the couch placed beside the machine.

"Ok tell me how are feeling right now?" Nysha maam quesioned.

"I'm feeling good, perfect, in fact fully energized," Rajveer said.

"And what is going on in your mind in this particular moment?" Nysha maam asked again.

"Frankly speaking Nysha Ji, right now nothing is going on in my mind; I'm just fully indulged in exercise today. Actually I'm enjoying it, I'm doing the exercise which I love, I've music of my taste with me. So right now I don't need any third person or any thought to capture my mind," Rajveer clarified.

Nysha maam smiled.

"Why are you smiling?" Rajveer asked.

"You know Rajveer there are certain people who are actually diamond, they've got everything but the only person is; they don't know that they are a diamond," Nysha maam said.

Rajveer looked puzzled as if what Nysha maam was trying to explain.

She further continued, "You are one of those people who is capable of doing everything, you are a DIAMOND (putting pressure on this word) and you just need a master to polish you and make you worth of what you are."

"You mean to say that I'm a diamond and you're a master," he said.

"Yes you can say that," she responded.

"Ok it's good to know that I'm a diamond. So which lesson will polish me today?" Rajveer grinned.

"Today we'll learn from your exercise session," she said.

"Exercise session?" Rajveer baffled.

What've happened to Nysha maam? Earlier she was asking questions like she was the host of KBC, then said Rajveer a diamond and now learning from exercise session? I don't know what she was saying but she has her own way of getting things understood.

"Can you please elaborate?" Rajveer requested.

"Now listen to me carefully," she said looking directly into the eyes of Rajveer, "right now you're doing the thing which you love the most and I can see the spark in your eyes. You are fully energized and radiating. You're actually feeling good from within."

Nisha Paryani Sharma

"Yes I know this but what is the point to emphasize on it again?" Rajveer asked continuing doing his exercise on the machine.

"The point is Mr. Rajveer, if we do all the activities which we love irrespective of the current situation or other people's interest or doing it just for the sake of doing it; our life will be fun," she further continued, "There is a saying about this which says if you do the work you love; you'll never have to work for a single day."

"Now you've a point," Rajveer conceded.

"To live life like a king size; you've to follow what your heart and mind says. You have to find a reason to live; a reason which your heart follows," Nysha maam said cheerfully.

What is my reason to live? My mind was thinking.

"For that I've to think what my heart and mind says," Rajveer said idly.

"Relax. Don't do it now. Go home, take a bath, sit all alone, take a pen and paper and then listen to your heart and mind and then make a list of all those things you love to do," Nysha maam responded.

"I've one question to ask Nysha Ji?" Rajveer said.

"Yes please say it," Nysha maam said smiling.

"I'll do all these things what you're telling me; but ultimately after sometime my past comes in front of me. And at times I curse my life and at times feel completely lost as if why it'd happened with me," Rajveer choked and he left the machine and sat beside Nysha maam on the couch.

"Listen Rajveer, remember these things whenever you get such a feeling.

1. We can't change our past but learn from it.
2. Whatever is happening with us; is for a very good reason.
3. Change your outlook towards everything and see it as an opportunity rather than a problem.
4. Accept the change that is coming into your life." Nysha maam stated.

That is a good piece of suggestion. If I will apply this thing to me in every situation; I guess I'll get lesser problems and more happiness.

"It seems simple to do but it's not easy," Rajveer objected.

"See, again this is your perspective and negative thoughts towards it. Give it a chance and please change your thinking," Nysha maam reiterated.

Rajveer said nothing and looked down.

"Cheer up Rajveer, don't get upset. It isn't that difficult and afterall you're doing it for yourself," Nysha maam said generously.

Rajveer looked up into the eyes of Nysha maam and that time he can see her twinkling eyes with full of spark.

"So what I'm supposed to do with the list?" he asked.

"Now that you've the list of things you love to do, read them again and again and prioritize them," Nysha maam mentioned.

"Prioritize?" Rajveer bewildered.

"Yes prioritize them which meant put first things first. Take up that activity which is more important to you which fills you with joy and you get pleasure while doing it. Rate the activities on the list from 1 to 10 and then do it. Put all your focus on to it and finish it; no matter whatever time it takes," Nysha maam explained.

"Hmmmm" Rajveer said nothing except it.

Today when I'll go home, I'll shake my brain and make a list of my loving activities and would definitely do them. I was getting eager to do it. It looked like a fun to me. By doing this I'll get to know more about myself as if what I like or love to do.

"I'm sure you're going to do this," Nysha maam promped.

"Yes of course I'll do it." Rajveer confirmed her.

At last Nysha maam said one last thing and she stood up to go back home and she said, "This life is very beautiful Rajveer, it is the gift of GOD; so enjoy it in every moment and don't waste it by doing or thinking unnecessary things because ultimately it's not the years that are counted; it is the life in those years that is counted."

And Nysha maam left from there and Rajveer was still sitting pondering on what Nysha maam has just said.

CHAPTER: 8

Life Is Once, So Live It Today

*"There are only 2 ways to live your life.
One is as though nothing is a miracle. The
other is as though everything is a miracle."*
— *Albert Einstein*

Life is beautiful and yet life is not a bed of roses. Though it is full of ups and downs it has many facets of blessings and successes. To some people life is very hard, harsh and cruel to them. They take life as a punishment for them as they never get what they want. These people always believe that there is no place for them in this life and they are a mere shit on earth and whatever they do can never be good. Still there are few more people who feel delighted in committing crimes and hurting people, to them life is a curse and they don't have any direction or aim in life to move further. They are living because they've got a human body to live. While there is another set of people who see life as a blessing, as a challenge, as a way to innovation and creating wealth and achieve great success. To them life is beautiful, colorful and cheerful. Whatever comes in their way let it be good or bad; they embrace it with open arms and learn to proceed further with a more positive thinking. Such kind of people create positive aura around themselves which then transfers their positive energy into their surroundings.

Life given by GOD is same for all; it's up to you how you take it. Either you face it or make it. It's up to you to take life as an opportunity to achieve all your goals and live it to the fullest with full satisfaction or take your life as miserable journey where nothing belongs to you and only fate is the master of your life. Everybody on this planet should live for a reason, a reason to make their parents happy, a reason to live a lavish life, a reason to achieve the targets, a reason to pass all the exams of life, a reason to attain high level of spirituality, a reason to get what you want. And for anyone to succeed in life, he should live with a reason with a purpose and must show all his capability and ability of what he has. He must be ready to sacrifice his time and put his 100% energy towards his goal. No matter what other's say about you, it's only you know where you want to go and what you'll achieve.

Life is so easy; yet many people rush here and there and miss what they want to accomplish in life. Don't rush in life. Take one step at a time. Each step should be properly planned before moving head. Steady, balance, mark and shoot. A journey of a thousand miles begins with one step. Take it.

❧ ✣ ☙

STORY: *Enjoy Your Life At Every Moment*

Once a fisherman was sitting near seashore under the shadow of a tree smoking his beedi. Suddenly a rich businessman passing by approached him and enquired as to why he was sitting under a tree smoking and not working. To this the poor fisherman replied that he had caught enough fishes for the day.

Hearing this; the rich man got angry and said: Why don't you catch more fishes instead of sitting in shadow wasting your time?

Fisherman asked: What would I do by catching more fishes?
Businessman: You could catch more fishes, sell them and earn more money, and buy a bigger boat.
Fisherman: What would I do then?
Businessman: You could go fishing in deep waters and catch even more fishes and earn even more money.
Fisherman: What would I do then?
Businessman: You could buy many boats and employ many people to work for you and earn even more money.
Fisherman: What would I do then?
Businessman: You could become a rich businessman like me.
Fisherman: What would I do then?
Businessman: You could then enjoy your life peacefully.
Fisherman: What do you think I'm doing right now?

MORAL—You don't need to wait for tomorrow to be happy and enjoy your life. You don't even need to be richer, more powerful to enjoy life. LIFE is at this moment, enjoy it fully. As some great men have said "My riches consist not in extent of my possessions but in the fewness of my wants".

What Do You See? What's Your Spotlight On? Problem or Opportunity?

I remember one day I was at home and it was raining heavily. I was feeling very hungry at that time and suddenly lights went off. I immediately searched for a torch and went in to the kitchen to search out some stuff or eatable to eat. For a moment I was blank as if what to do now but thanks to the inventor of life and the one who made torch who didn't allowed me to stay hungry and get what I wanted. The torch has its ability to highlight a single person, object or anything that is needed keeping the rest in darkness or out of the focus. Similarly each one of us has an in built torch in our conscious mind. It is called attention. The trouble is we focus our attention on what is wrong in life keeping everything Ok aside in the darkness. Everywhere we see people focus only on the problem; newspapers and television channels tells only about inflation, corruption etc, young men and women always talk about betrayal of their love, some have problem in their personal and professional careers, kids have arrogance towards their studies, older people arc worried about their health.

Everybody has one thing in common—their focus on the problem. It is not wrong that you focus on your problem but what is more essential is to take one step ahead to find out the solution of your problem and move your mental attention towards the solution. There will be always some or the other problem in your life but how about turning your spotlight on to those joyous and happy occurrences in your life? Life will always present you with all kind of problem but it's up to you how you see the situation—as a problem or as an opportunity. Always remember problems will call for your attention from time to time; the trick is to know when to turn the spotlight away from them and on to something good.

STORY: *The Obstacle In Our Path*

In ancient times, a King had a boulder placed on a roadway. Then he hid himself and watched to see if anyone would remove the huge rock. Some of the king's wealthiest merchants and courtiers came by and simply walked around it. Many loudly blamed the King for not keeping the roads clear, but none did anything about getting the stone out of the way.

Then a peasant came along carrying a load of vegetables. Upon approaching the boulder, the peasant laid down his burden and tried to move the stone to the side of the road. After much pushing and straining, he finally succeeded. After the peasant picked up his load of vegetables, he noticed a purse lying in the road where the boulder had been. The purse contained many gold coins and a note from the King indicating that the gold was for the person who removed the boulder from the roadway.

The peasant learned what many of us never understand! Every obstacle presents an opportunity to improve our condition.

Love Your Life

STORY: God's Coffee

A group of alumni, highly established in their careers, got together to visit their old university professor. Conversation soon turned into complaints about stress in work and life.

Offering his guests coffee, the professor went to the kitchen and returned with a large pot of coffee and an assortment of cups—porcelain, plastic, glass, crystal, some plain looking, some

expensive, some exquisite—telling them to help themselves to the coffee.

When all the students had a cup of coffee in hand, the professor said:

"If you noticed, all the nice looking expensive cups were taken up, leaving behind the plain and cheap ones. While it is normal for you to want only the best for yourselves, that is the source of your problems and stress.

Be assured that the cup itself adds no quality to the coffee. In most cases it is just more expensive and in some cases even hides what we drink.

What all of you really wanted was coffee, not the cup, but you consciously went for the best cups . . . And then you began eyeing each other's cups.

Now consider this: Life is the coffee; the jobs, money and position in society are the cups. They are just tools to hold and contain Life, and the type of cup we have does not define, nor change the quality of Life we live.

Sometimes, by concentrating only on the cup, we fail to enjoy the coffee God has provided us."

God brews the coffee, not the cups . . . . Enjoy your coffee!

It's very common now-a-days that people rush for materialistic things and don't look inside what they're missing. In the hunt for earning more money, get a promotion, achieve high targets, people fail to enjoy the basic happiness of their life and when they grew old they curse their life and themselves to have lost all those golden days, like bunking a class in the school, spending a day with their grand parents, eating a pani puri at road side, dancing in the rain, attending the annual function of their kids, watching your child while receiving award and many more. At the end, people stay all alone leaving aside no memories of joy but only the harshness of their boss, their job, their unsuccessful life etc. But there is always never late in starting a new beginning.

As Maria Robinson says, "Nobody can go back and start a new beginning, but anyone can start today and make a new ending." Stop running towards materialistic life and start moving toward your soul, toward the ultimate happiness. Make a call to your friend to say he is special for you, give a hug to your neighbor and say I belong to you, learn a lesson in life each day that you live, make every day count, appreciate every moment and take from those moments everything that you possibly can, for you may never be able to experience it again, listen to people what they have to say, forgive people around you, help the needy people, see every people as an opportunity, don't procrastinate, take actions and move ahead. For this, it will make you happy from within and also to the people around you. At the end, you will be satisfied with your life for such small and great works you did even if you're not getting pension, even if you're ill, even if you're alone but you're happy from within. You have all those good memories with you which nobody can steal from you. Enjoy your life and live it to the fullest.

> *"You've gotta dance like there's nobody watching,*
> *Love like you'll never b hurt,*

Sing like there's nobody listening,
And live like it's heaven on earth."
—*William W. Purkey*

Know Who You Are? Identify Yourself.

STORY: How Would You Like To Be Remembered?

About a hundred years ago, a man looked at the morning newspaper and to his surprise and horror, read his name in the obituary column. The news papers had reported the death of the wrong person by mistake. His first response was shock. Am I here or there? When he regained his composure, his second thought was to find out what people had said about him. The obituary read, "Dynamite King Dies." And also "He was the merchant of death." This man was the inventor of dynamite and when he read the words "merchant of death," he asked himself a question, "Is this how I am going to be remembered?" He got in touch with his feelings and decided that this was not the way he wanted to be remembered. From that day on, he started working toward peace. His name was Alfred Nobel and he is remembered today by the great Nobel Prize. Just as Alfred Nobel got in touch with his feelings and redefined his values, we should step back and do the same.

"Life isn't about finding yourself. Life is about creating you." says George Bernard Shaw. There are thousands of people who live life like Alfred lived earlier. People are just living because they have to live without even knowing the purpose of life. Have you ever thought why this human life is given to you? Have you ever given a thought of what is the sole purpose of your life? Ask yourself; what is it that is best in you, what skills and talent makes you different from others, what is that 1 best quality which makes you stand out of the crowd. Find it, know it, polish it and make it your USP. Once you've identified your skill start working on it, start sharpening the saw before cutting the tree. Be the master of that skill that no one else can stand in front of you. You and only you are the master and it's you who had conquered the skill. And once you'll achieve it, get to know about it thoroughly, all conditions will be in your favor. You'll se the difference and then you can move your life the way you wanted, you'll be able to change the situation in whichever direction you want as beautifully described in the following story.

STORY: The Carrot, The Egg, and The Coffee Bean

A young woman went to her mother and told her about her life and how things were so hard for her. She did not know how she was going to make it and wanted to give up. She was tired of fighting and struggling.

It seemed that, as one problem was solved, a new one arose. Her mother took her to the kitchen. She filled three pots with water and placed each on a high fire. Soon the pots came to a boil. In the first, she placed carrots, in the second she placed eggs, and in the last she placed ground coffee beans.

She let them sit and boil, without saying a word. In about twenty minutes, she turned off the burners. She fished the carrots out and placed them in a bowl. She pulled the eggs out and placed them in a bowl. Then she ladled the coffee out and placed it in a bowl. Turning to her daughter, she asked, "Tell me, what you see?"

"Carrots, eggs, and coffee," the young woman replied. The mother brought her closer and asked her to feel the carrots. She did and noted that they were soft. She then asked her to take an egg and break it. After pulling off the shell, she observed the hard-boiled egg. Finally, she asked her to sip the coffee. The daughter smiled as she tasted its rich aroma. The daughter then asked, "What does it mean, mother?"

Her mother explained that each of these objects had faced the same adversity—boiling water—but each reacted differently. The carrot went in strong, hard and unrelenting. However, after being subjected to the boiling water, it softened and became weak.

The egg had been fragile. Its thin outer shell had protected its liquid interior. But, after sitting through the boiling water, its inside became hardened! The ground coffee beans were unique, however. After they were in the boiling water, they had changed the water.

"Which are you?" the mother asked her daughter. "When adversity knocks on your door, how do you respond? Are you a carrot, an egg, or a coffee bean?" Think of this: Which am I? Am I the carrot that seems strong but, with pain and adversity, do I wilt and become soft and lose my strength? Am I the egg that starts with a malleable heart, but changes with the heat? Did I have a fluid spirit but, after a death, a breakup, or a financial hardship, does my shell look the same, but on the inside am I bitter and tough with a stiff spirit and a hardened heart? Or am I like the coffee bean? The bean actually changes the hot water, the very circumstance that brings the pain. When the water gets hot, it releases the fragrance and flavor.

If you are like the bean, when things are at their worst, you get better and change the situation around you. When the hours are the darkest and trials are their greatest, do you elevate to another level? How do you handle adversity? Are you a carrot, an egg, or a coffee bean?

What is your Priority? Put First Things First.

> *"Most of us spend too much time on what is urgent and not enough time on what is important."*
> —*Stephen R. Covey*

I've heard people saying, "I want to do this or I want to achieve something big." let it be money, job, status or any relationship. Everybody is running after one or the other thing. But the big question is; are they running for the right thing? Is it worth their life? Does it add any meaning to their life? Such questions remain unanswerable. In one day, a person has thousands of tasks to do and one actually does such thousands of tasks but what matters most is do they do the things which are more important or they are just doing for the sake of doing. People live their life because they'd been given a life without any dream, a vision or a goal. Even if they have dream, they didn't know how to make it real.

> *"It's not enough to be busy, so are the ants. The question is; what are we busy about?"*
> —*Henry David Thoreau*

Now that we have encountered with the problem, let's come to its solution. To live a joyful life, to achieve your goal and to make your dream real, one has to prioritize his work, one has to do the essentials and remove non essential work. As rightly said by Tin Yu tang, "Besides the noble art of getting things done, there is the noble art of leaving things undone. The wisdom in life consists in the elimination of non-essentials." It is not necessary that daily we have to work or do the things which we usually use to do. Eliminate those unnecessary things from your life and make a schedule of your most important things and then prioritize your schedule and follow what Lee Iacoca says, "If you want to make good use of your time, you've got to know what's most important and then give it what all you've got."

Practical Tip:

1. Take a piece of paper and write down your dream.
2. Divide your dream into small goals.
3. Write down the tasks involved in accomplishing those goals.
4. Do a self analysis over the tasks written.
5. Ask yourself what value does each task adds to fulfill your goal
6. Remove the unnecessary tasks.
7. Now write down the remaining tasks.
8. And most importantly prioritize these tasks to achieve your goal, to reach to your dream.

[Note: while removing the tasks always remember one thing said by Albert Einstein, "Not everything that can be counted counts and not everything that counts can be counted."]

STORY

A professor stood before his philosophy class and had some items in front of him. When the class began, wordlessly, he picked up a very large and empty jar and proceeded to fill it with golf balls. He then asked the students if the jar was full. They agreed that it was. So the professor then picked up a box of small pebbles and poured them into the jar. He shook the jar lightly. The pebbles rolled into the open areas between the golf balls. He then asked the students again if the jar was full. They agreed it was.

The professor next picked up a box of sand and poured it into the jar. Of course, the sand filled up everything else. He asked once more if the jar was full. The students responded with a unanimous "Yes." The professor then produced two cans of coco from under the table and poured the entire contents into the jar, effectively filling the empty space between the sand. The students laughed.

"Now", said the professor, as the laughter subsided, "I want you to recognize that this jar represents your life. The golf balls are the important things—your family, your children, your health, your friends, your favorite passions—things that, if everything else was lost and only they remained, your life would still be full. The pebbles are the other things that matter like your job, your house, your car.

The sand is everything else—the small stuff. If you put the sand into the jar first" he continued, "there is no room for the pebbles or the golf balls. The same goes for life. If you spend all your time and energy on the small stuff, you will never have room for the things that are important to you. Pay attention to the things that are critical to your happiness. Play with your children. Take time to get medical checkups. Take your partner out to dinner. There will always be time to clean the house, and fix the rubbish. Take care of the golf balls first, the things that really matter. Set your priorities. The rest is just sand".

One of the students raised her hand and inquired what the coco represented. The professor smiled. "I'm glad you asked. It just goes to show you that, no matter how full your life may seem, there's always room for a couple of coco".

"Things which matter most must never be at the mercy of things which matter least."
—Johann Wolfgang von Goetha

CHAPTER 9

Accept the Change

*"God grant me the serenity to accept the
things I cannot change, the courage to
change the things I can, and the wisdom to
know the difference."*

—Reinhold Neibuhr

C hange is something which occurs constantly
and continuously. Change is like time which
never stops. Each and every day change comes in our
life with a new reformed identity. Every day every
moment our body composition is changing. Metabolism
is occurring at cellular level and regularly new cells are
forming while old tissues are dying. Change occurs not
only on physical level but simultaneously on mental and
psychological levels too. As we grew up, our mental
level changes, we begin to adopt new things, adopt new
ideas, new creations and our attitude towards every little
thing changes as we grew older. Like one says while
childhood we see Mama in the moon while in adulthood

the same moon becomes our lover. So our attitude has changed.

Life is neither constant nor the same. It is ever changing. Life brings to us many of wanted and unwanted changes to ourselves. Some of the events make us happy while some of them takes away the smile from our face and makes us sad. Every event whether good or bad definitely brings certain change, yet how many of us embrace and welcome change. When change is good, we feel good but when change is bad, why do we curse it? We cannot avoid change; it has to come so why do many of us resist it? Why do we feel safe when we have a stable job? A stable marriage? Or a stable circle of friends? Why can't we open ourselves and our mind to the new ideas, new situations and new change? There is nothing wrong to feel safe in your comfort zone but it is definitely wrong to feel threatened when change comes knocking at our door. Why one is scared to go to one city and do job? Why one doesn't want transfer? Why one doesn't accept the harshness life had given? While we go through tough times, always remember it's just a part of a life. If it has come, it has to go also. It will not remain forever. So why not enjoy even in that change. Many of us are scared from change.

The only certainty in life is uncertainty. The only constant in life is constant change. We value comfort, stability and certainty, and yet these things don't really exist. This can cause some people stress, as they worry about what is going to happen to them. A better strategy would be to re-orient your thinking so that you not only value change, but embrace it as a healthy and important part of your life.

171

It is change that allows new opportunities to reveal themselves to us. It is change that allows us to be creative. It is change that heals sickness. It is change that allows us to try different things. It is change that encourages us to adopt new life strategies. It is change that allows us to take on new skills. It is change that allows us to change our beliefs. Change can and should be a very positive dynamic in our life.

There are some people who seem to choose to stay where they are. According to them something known is better for them than something big scary unknown. But what if the unknown is better than the known? What if the unknown brings more happiness in your life? While on the other hand, there are some people who love and accept the change. Whatever life throws at them, they embrace it with full grace and go with the flow. Everyday you can make a choice. You can remain where you are or choose to move forward and try something new. You can shut the door for new opportunities or welcome it with open arms. You can be "safe" in your present or take a "risk" to make your future better and more exciting. Whatever you chose, you cannot avoid change at all, it has to and it will definitely come. It's up to you how you take it. The trick is to become aware of change as it happens and adopt yourself in such a manner that it serves your purpose. It's up to you to go with the flow or fight against the waves.

> **"Be the change that you wish to see in the world."**
> —*Mahatma Gandhi*

It's Your Choice

It's always your wish how you want to live your life. Any day you can wish to adopt yourself to new change. Any day you can wish to start a new activity. Any day you can wish to start reading a new book to enhance your knowledge. Any day you can wish to learn something new or you can also do nothing. It's all your choice. You can choose rest over labour, comfort over uneasiness, entertainment over education, past over future, doubt over confidence. But always remember, whatever you choose it'll be your choice. You are responsible for your circumstances. You have the ability and responsibility to make better choices. Also if you don't like how things are, change it. You are not a tree. You have the ability to transform your life and it begins with your very own choice. As Greek philosopher Heraclitus has said, "You cannot get into the same river twice." The flow of water ensures that. It's constantly changing, just as you are. For like the flowing river, you too are not the same person. Your body, your thoughts, your beliefs, your observations, your perception, attitude, everything is changing as river's water.

> *"The snake which cannot cast its skin has to die. As well the minds which are prevented from changing their opinion, they cease to be mind."*
>
> —*Friedrich Nietzsche*

Talking too much about change, it reminds me of a story I've read a few days back. It is one of book which grabbed my attention. I was just collecting books for my library where suddenly I read the title of this book and that moment I'd decided, I'll read this book and the very next day I read it, complete it and adopt the lessons in my own life. The book is "Who Moved My Cheese?" by Spencer Johnson. There are plenty of lessons one can draw from this simple story. And the story goes like this:

It revolves around four characters and loads of cheese hidden in different parts of a maze. The four characters are very cleverly named so as to judge their attitudes and characteristics: **Sniff, Scurry, Hem and Haw**. First two are mice and the latter two are small people, as depicted by the author. They move around the maze for cheese to feed on. They also land at a cheese station full of cheese. So full, they think it is enough to last a life time. In life's way, suddenly all the cheese disappears from that station, leaving the four stunned. The reality is, it had been gradually decreasing, but they had failed to foresee it. How they react to this situation is the remaining part of the story; the best part of the story.

Cheese here, is not cheese as it sounds, but a metaphor that stands for things we pursue in life. A job, a relationship, money or any material for that matter. Cheese can even be an activity which we cannot do without doing. The cheese having disappeared implies change. Change of a routine which hits us right in the face when we least expect it to.

Sniff and Scurry are mice with a smaller brain than humans. Naturally, we tend to think they are less intelligent than human beings. But in reality, smaller brain implies lesser complexity; fewer rules to follow;

faster decisions. Sniff is good at "sniffing out" cheese, and Scurry excels at "scurrying" after the cheese once he knows where it is. The two mice don't really think about things. They just react to them. They find cheese; they eat cheese. They don't find it; they go places, looking for it. Unlike us, they don't over-analyze and waste time doing paperback calculations. They don't plan. They act. Spontaneously act. And most of the time, it is what works well. Sniff and Scurry are ready to handle the cheese crisis. They, without second thoughts, get back to looking for more.

Hem and Haw, you could say, are a little bit too complicated than the simple mice. They can't help using their brains more because they have them. Hem, in particular and as the name suggests, is someone who is afraid of change; one who cannot take a break from the routine. Is this not the situation in which we find ourselves most of the time? It might even be too late before the estimation and other careful planning are done. The hesitation to move on and the lame reasons we state in defense are also brought out pretty well.

The two little people, however, mope around, blaming someone for moving their cheese. They claim they don't deserve to be in such a situation because they worked hard through the maze to find that cheese. They are not prepared to look again for more, even though it is their only source of survival. At an instance, even after Haw came over his fear, laughed at himself for being so foolish and moved on without Hem, Hem stays stubbornly put, insisting that someone will put his cheese back. Haw, on his way, scribbles on walls for Hem to know the way, just in case he changed his mind and decided to follow him. These scribbling are the goods the author wants to deliver. To make a long story short, (I know I could have done it in the first place, but still . . .)

1. They keep moving the cheese. (Change happens)
2. Get ready for the cheese to move. (Anticipate change)
3. Smell the cheese often, so you know when it's getting old. (Monitor change)
4. The quicker you let go of old cheese, the sooner you can enjoy new cheese. (Adapt to change quickly)
5. Move with the cheese. (Change)36
6. Savour the adventure and enjoy the taste of new cheese. (Enjoy change)
7. Someone will keep moving the cheese. (Be ready to enjoy change quickly, and enjoy it every time)

Both, in this narration and in reality, the end of the story is always in favour of the daring, Sniff, Scurry and Haw. Ask yourself, "What would I do if I were not afraid?", and get going, because a "good enough" solution to a problem is fine; much better in fact than a "no-solution". Even the best would be futile if it comes all the late.

7th Meeting

Tring Tring.

"Hello," Nysha maam said.

"Maam, Mr. Rajveer has come," the receptionist of Nysha maam's office said.

"Tell him to wait Nancy if he can; as I'm very busy today," Nysha maam replied and hung up the phone.

"Maam is very busy today so you can wait if you want," the receptionist Nancy said to Rajveer.

Listening to this Rajveer got nervous. He was looking confused; little lost and was sweating too. And why he should not; he was 2 hours late today.

Nysha maam had fixed up the meeting at 9:00 am but for some reason (Rajveer's favourite traffic jam) he didn't came on time.

And now he was nervous because he had repeated the same mistake many times and this time it was too late. It was 11: 30 am by now when Rajveer reached Nysha maam's office.

"I hope Nysha maam is not angry with me," Rajveer was thinking in his mind.

Rajveer was moving here and there in the lobby and was waiting for Nysha maam's call.

After some time he sat on the sofa placed in the lobby.

This is your punishment Rajveer for coming late. Every time Nysha maam will not excuse you. My mind was saying.

At 1:00 pm Rajveer stood up and went up to the reception and asked Nancy, "How much more time will Nysha Ji take? Please tell her that I'm waiting."

Nancy nodded and took up the receiver and dialed the intercom number.

"Yes Nancy," Nysha maam said.

"Maam Mr. Rajveer is still here and waiting for your call."

"Oh! He is still here," Nysha maam said shockingly, "Tell him to go home and have lunch as I'll be free after 5: 00 pm and if he can come; tell him to meet me after 5.00 pm OK."

"Ok maam," Nancy replied and put down the phone and gave the message to Rajveer.

Rajveer beseeched Nancy to call Nysha maam again and meet him now but Nancy refused to do so and it was already told to Nancy not to disturb her again and again.

Rajveer felt disgusting, put his head down and moved out from the office.

Time ran quickly for Nysha maam but slowly for Rajveer.

Nysha maam was busy dealing with her clients while Rajveer went out, had a lunch and was completely free now and was wandering as if what to do and where to go. He didn't even go back to his home.

And at 4: 30 pm, he was back at Nysha maam's office. He came quietly and sat on the sofa and signaled Nancy in his gestures that he has come.

After about 40 minutes Nysha maam came out from her room. She was wearing purple and light pink salwar kurta and her hairs were open. She was carrying a little bag on her right shoulder with car keys in her hand.

I guess she was about to leave the office and had completely forgot about Rajveer's meeting.

As soon as she came out, Rajveer stood up and came near to her and said, "Hii Good evening Nysha Ji."

Nysha maam was shocked to see Rajveer over there as she didn't expect him till this time. "Oh Rajveer . . . . . . Good evening . . . . You're still here. Were you waiting since morning?" Nysha maam asked surprisingly.

"Yes I'm waiting but in the middle I went out to have lunch and then came back," Rajveer quivered.

Nysha maam was till shocked and can't believe that Rajveer was waiting since he has always allotted this waiting job to Nysha maam.

"Look Rajveer sorry for letting you wait but I was very busy today and right now also I've to reach my home and have got some work today," Nysha maam said politely and both of them started moving outside the lobby and stood in front of the lift.

Why Nysha maam is saying sorry. If I would have been in her place, I would have ignored him and even didn't talk to him but this is Nysha maam; so polite and so generous.

"Why are you saying sorry to me? In fact it was my entire mistake and I'm really sorry for coming late," Rajveer trembled.

"Don't make it your habit of coming late," Nysha maam stated and she continued, "Anyways by the time I'll reach home you can come with me in my car. I suppose my driving time can be used to talk with you; isn't it?"

"Whatever you say Nysha Ji," Rajveer replied.

Both of them entered the lift, she pressed the underground floor button and lift started moving downwards. In the lift no one talked.

The lift door opened and Nysha maam preceded towards her car, unlocked it, and seated inside and Rajveer also sat in the front seat.

"So, traffic jam hmmm?" Nysha maam scoffed and the silence broke.

"Not this time. Actually last night I was watching movie and I didn't remember when I fall asleep and I forget to put the alarm and in the morning when I woke up, I saw the time and I just ran to come over here," Rajveer reasoned.

"This is not expected from you Rajveer. I thought you're a good boy," she said and started the car and put her leg on the accelerator and within a minute the car was on road now.

"I'm sorry Nysha Ji, I'm really sorry," Rajveer pleaded.

"Don't say sorry again and again. Just be on time and you don't have to feel embarrassed in front of me," she said and Rajveer nodded.

"Time is very precious to me Rajveer and I hope it is priceless for every one. Once gone it'll never come back and also the things will never come back which had passed through the time," Nysha maam said in agony.

Rajveer looked at Nysha maam at his right side and was trying to understand what she was saying.

"If a doctor comes late only by few minutes, the heart patient can die in OT; if a student enters late in exam hall, he can loose his 1 whole year. And you know because of this habit of coming late; I'd lost my husband," Nysha maam almost squeaked.

Rajveer again looked at Nysha maam but this time he was completely shocked.

What? Nysha maam had lost her husband. My mind did not believe this statement of her.

Rajveer gathered enough courage to speak and asked, "How did it happen?"

"That day he'd an important meeting with company's board of directors; and as usual he woke up late like all other days and when he reminded about the meeting, he gets fussy and rushed for everything and only stopped when he'd a car accident and was dead on the spot," Nysha maam panicked while saying as if the incident was happening in front of her eyes.

Rajveer also shivered but tried to control his emotions and consoled Nysha maam and said, "I'm sorry for this."

Nysha maam didn't noticed what Rajveer was saying. She was in her own and continued saying, "That time I was thinking if Punit would have woke up early or had not the habit of procrastination; he would not have that accident and today he would be alive there for me."

Rajveer said nothing but was only listening to what she was saying.

I don't know what had happened to her. She was talking as if no one is there. She was completely lost in her own and was deeply missing her husband.

After a while she returned her consciousness and realized that now he is gone forever. She looked at Rajveer and said, "Value your time Rajveer, if once it goes it'll never come back. You can witness it by today's incident; you came late today and your whole day was wasted. I know this is not a big issue for you but when these habits grow up, it may cause a disaster."

Rajveer didn't know what to say. He had already said sorry many times for his mistake. Still he'd to say something, "I'm really sorry Nysha Ji, I'll not be late in future anytime; I promise."

"I hope you keep your promise," Nysha maam prompted.

"Definitely I will," he replied.

The conversation was over and Nysha maam reached her destination.

Rajveer opened the car gate and was about to step out but stopped by her words, "This time is very important Rajveer, we always run for the things we don't have. When we were kids, we wanted to be adults and when we become adults we want to be kid again. When we were bachelors, we wanted to marry and when we get married, we miss our bachelor's life and want to live like that again; but that doesn't seems to happen. So why can't we enjoy this very moment. We don't know what will happen next, a joyous moment or a tragedy; but we know today and make it better by utilizing our time in right direction. Just value your time and the time will value you in future."

Nysha mam's words were bouncing in my mind. This actually happens with me. Rather than living in this present moment, I always think of what will happen next; and in the lust of better future, I forget to enjoy the present moment.

CHAPTER 10

Value Your Time

"Time is free, but it's priceless. You can't own it, but you can use it. You can't keep it, but you can spend it. Once you've lost it, you can never get it back."

—*Harvey Mackay*

It's very often to hear from people saying, "I couldn't do that work because I don't have time", I'll not attend the party because I don't have time." Husband says to wife, "We can't go for vacation because I don't have time." A father says to his son, "I can't come to attend your annual function since I've a meeting and no time left for school function." People are very busy with their schedule; they are busy in their offices and business. They don't have a little time for their friends, family, and relatives. They don't even have time for themselves. They are just running without knowing the final destination. Such people are running on the road which leads nowhere. The vision, the goal, the ultimate success is missing from their life.

They don't spend time with their kids, with friends or with nature. They can take out time for other wrong activities like smoking, late night parties, pornography etc. but not a single day dedicated completely to their grandparents or their family. And when asked to them, why do you live such stressful life and don't enjoy; they complain that they don't have time. But the fact is all of us have time; even the one who has nothing else has time. As H.Jackson Brown says, "Don't say you don't have enough time. You have exactly the same number of hours per day that were given to Hellen Keller, Pasteur, Michaelangelo, Mother Teresa, Leonarda da Vinci, Thomas Jefferson and Albert Einstien."

As we go through life, we realize for ourselves that if there is anything in the world which will never come back, it is time. Once time passes away, it becomes past and then it will never return to present. Time is the most precious thing one can ever have; it is more precious than money. Money can buy everything but not time. Time waits for none. It comes and goes. Those who do not understand the value of time will waste it or spend it doing nothing. There is a proverb which says, "Killing time is not a murder; it is a suicide." It means by wasting time one is not harming others rather he is harming himself. As Stephen R. Covey says, "The key is not in spending time, but in investing it."

There are certain people who are very busy, they have a busy schedule as going to work from 7 in morning to 5 in evening, coming home and have dinner with family, watch some TV, do some paper work then going to bed at 11 at night and again wake up at 6 am next morning. And there are also some people who work and study, spend time with parents, and play for some time with their kids. These are the people who are actually utilizing the time to its fullest.

But there are some people who are just couch potatoes. They'll wake up in morning at 11, eat brunch (breakfast + lunch), watch some movie or TV, surf on net; again eat something. By that time they're tired and went back to sleep again for 1 or 2 hours, wake up and call friends, go for a party, have their dinner outside, come home at late nights, again watch movie at sleep at around 2 or 3 in the morning. Such people don't take time seriously because its not money. Now-a-days it's only money which means everything to people. But one must remember that time is more powerful than money. With 10 hours of work, one can get Rs.100 worth on money. But with Rs.100, one cannot get 10 hours of his/her life. Those 10 hours are gone forever. Time can create us or destroy us. It all depends on how we utilize time.

> *"Time is really the only capital that any human being has, and the only thing he can't afford to lose."*
> —*Thomas Edison*

Imagine there is a bank that credits your account each morning with Rs.86,400. It carries over no balance from day to day. Every evening the bank deletes whatever part of the balance you failed to use during the day. What would you do? Draw out every cent, of course! Each of us has such a bank. Its name is TIME. Every morning, it credits you with 86,400 seconds. Every night it writes off, as lost, whatever of this you have failed to invest to good purpose. It carries over no balance. It allows no overdraft. Each day it opens a new account for you. Each night it burns the remains of the day. If you fail to use the day's deposits, the loss is yours. There is no going back. There is no drawing against the "tomorrow." You must live in the present on today's deposits. Invest it so as to get from it the utmost in health, happiness, and success! The clock is running. Make the most of today. To realize the value of ONE YEAR, ask a student who failed a grade. To realize the value of ONE MONTH, ask a mother who gave birth to a premature baby. To realize the value of ONE WEEK, ask the editor of a weekly newspaper. To realize the value of ONE HOUR, ask the lovers who are waiting to meet. To realize the value of ONE MINUTE, ask a person who missed the train. To realize the value of ONE-SECOND, ask a person who just avoided an accident. To realize the value of ONE MILLISECOND—Ask the person who has won a silver medal in the Olympics. Treasure every moment that you have! And treasure it more because you shared it with someone special, special enough to spend your time. Remember that time waits for no one. Yesterday is history. Tomorrow is mystery. Today is a gift. That's why it's called the present!

> *"Each hour of this day will I cherish for it can never return. Each minute of this day will I grasp with both hands and fondle with love for its value is beyond price. What dying man can purchase another breath though he willingly gives all his gold? What price dare I place on the hours ahead? I*

**will make them priceless! I will live this day
as if it is my last."**

— *Og Mandino*

STORY: 1000 Marbles

2 friends were talking wih each other.
"Well, Tom, it sure sounds like you're busy with your job. I'm sure they pay you well but it's a shame you have to be away from home and your family so much. Hard to believe a young fellow should have to work sixty or seventy hours a week to make ends meet. Too bad you missed your daughter's dance recital."

He continued, "Let me tell you something Tom, something that has helped me keep a good perspective on my own priorities."

And that's when he began to explain his theory of a "thousand marbles." "You see, I sat down one day and did a little arithmetic. The average person lives about seventy-five years. I know, some live more and some live less, but on average, folks live about seventy-five years."
"Now then, I multiplied 75 times 52 and I came up with 3900 which is the number of Saturdays that the average person has in their entire lifetime. Now stick with me Tom, I'm getting to the important part."

"It took me until I was fifty-five years old to think about all this in any detail", he went on, "and by that time I

189

had lived through over 2800 Saturdays. I got to thinking that if I lived to be seventy-five, I only had about a 1000 of them left to enjoy."

So I went to a toy store and bought every single marble they had. I ended up having to visit three toy stores to round-up 1000 marbles. I took them home and put them inside of a large, clear plastic container right here in the shack next to my gear. Every Saturday since then, I have taken one marble out and thrown it away."

"I found that by watching the marbles diminish, I focused more on the really important things in life. There is nothing like watching your time here on this earth run out to help get your priorities straight."

"Now let me tell you one last thing before I go and take my lovely wife out for breakfast. This morning, I took the very last marble out of the container. I figure if I make it until next Saturday then I have been given a little extra time. And the one thing we can all use is a little more time." It was nice to meet you Tom, I hope you spend more time with your family, and I hope to meet you again.

You could have heard a pin drop when this fellow went away. I guess he gave us all a lot to think about. I had planned to work that morning. Instead, I went upstairs and woke my wife up with a kiss. "C'mon honey, I'm taking you and the kids to breakfast."

"What brought this on?" she asked with a smile. "Oh, nothing special, it's just been a while since we spent a

Saturday together with the kids. Hey, can we stop at a toy store while we're out? I need to buy some marbles."

This is an excellent way to make an abstract concept like time concrete. Of course you don't have to use marbles. You could use river gravel or pennies (just don't spend them).

I hope by now you must have understood what time really means and what time can give us what nobody else can give. Stop doing unnecessary things or unwanted things. Think on what your motive is and then spend your time on it and of course to your family too. Always remember God has given life to humans, animals and plants also but what is that unique thing we have what others don't have is our brain who can think, so engage your brain to think over it and spend your time smartly.

> **"It's not enough to be busy, so are the ants.**
> **The question is; what are we busy about?"**
> **—Henry David Thorean**

Think Over It!!!

8th Meeting

Somebody is at your doorstep, please open the door.
Somebody is at your doorstep, please open the door.
The door bell rang.

"I think she has come," Rajveer said and ran towards the door to open it.

"Welcome Nysha Ji, welcome to my home," Rajveer opened the door and greeted her with a big smile on his face.

Nysha maam entered, nodded and she also smiled.

She has a lovely smile, I must say.

Nysha maam was wearing patiala suit of pink, blue and yellow coloured combination. It looked as if there is a rainbow who'd taken a shape of a lady but she was looking stunning.

About 20 to 22 days after last meeting, today Rajveer had invited Nysha maam at his home over a coffee.

Both of them entered inside. After moving a few steps, there were 2 to 3 stairs to move down towards the lounge. Beautifully carved sofa set with furry carpet looked awesome. An antique glass painting on the wall had increased the value of the hall.

Rajveer signaled Nysha maam to move there and have a seat.

"You have a beautiful house Rajveer," Nysha maam complimented while looking all around.

"Thank you Nysha Ji," Rajveer replied.

"Welcome Nysha Ji," Rajveer's mother greeted Nysha maam.

She was sitting in the lounge and was waiting for her.

"Oh hello Aunti, How are you?" Nysha maam said.

"I'm all good. Please sit sit," replied Rajveer's mother.

All three of them settled and started chit chat.

Rajveer had talked to his mother last week and she had told her story to her son. The problem between both his father and mother is misunderstanding, ignoring each other or not giving time to each other. Actually Rajveer's father doesn't value her wife much and always compare her with all other staff and management ladies he works with. His father always tries to pull her down. Initially it was bearable to Rajveer's mother but later when his father turned violent and started beating his wife, she also get aggressive and lost her command. And the result is now both fights like dogs in the house.

Rajveer's mother had told everything about this to her son and now Rajveer understand her mother's situation; empathizes her but was also very angry. One because his father was beating his mother and second because his mother didn't told anything about this to her son.

Right now Rajveer's father is outside for a business tour and he and his mother had a deal to teach him a lesson.

Meanwhile the servant came in with plates of cookies and snacks with cups of coffee and placed it on the center table.

Rajveer had shared this matter with Nysha maam over telephone 3 days back and had invited her to his home.

"Please have some Nysha Ji," Rajveer's mother offered her the plate of cookies.

"Thank you Aunti," Nysha maam said and took one piece of cookie.

"So Rajveer, you are happy now?" Nysha maam asked.

"Yes I am, I'm very happy," Rajveer replied and hugged his mother sitting beside him.

"Rajveer today you are blushing," Nysha maam said huffily.

"So you must be thankful to me that you got your mother back," Nysha maam giggled.

"Nysha Ji, you know I'm extremely grateful to you," Rajveer replied.

"And to your mother . . . ." She said.

"Yes to her also," he said still in his hugging position.

"Mera raja beta," Rajveer's mother said while putting her right hand on his chin.

"And to GOD . . . . ." she said.

"Yes yes yes to Him also," he reiterated.

"Rajveer you must be thankful to everyone and for everything in your life," Nysha maam said.

"I don't know about everyone but yes I'm thankful to you and GOD that I got my mother back," Rajveer said exuberantly.

Rajveer's mother handed coffee cups to both Nysha maam and her son and she also took one.

"No it's not only I and GOD; be grateful to everyone like your barber who cut your hairs, your driver who drives for you, your servant who serves you, your neighbour's who took care of your mother in your absence, your friends who put proxy for your bunked class, your canteen owner who allowed you free snacks," Nysha maam mentioned.

"Yes beta, she is saying right," Rajveer's mother said.

Rajveer nodded and took the sip of coffee.

Nysha maam further continued and said, "and also be grateful for every big or small thing you have. If you have food in your fridge, clothes on your back, a roof over your head and a place to sleep; you are richer than 75% of the entire world. If you don't understand it, you are more fortunate than the 3 billion people in the world who cannot see, don't know English or suffer being mentally retarded. Life is not about exams, girl or guy who dumped you or whatever else that does not matter. It's about thousand other reasons to be happy and grateful."

What a thought? I never said thank you to GOD for such small things. Actually we people run for all materialistic things and forget that we are supplied with all basic necessities to survive and even more than that.

Thank you GOD that I've got everything to live my life in a healthy and happy way. I'm not deprived of anything. Thank you so much for your mercy upon me.

Rajveer looked puzzled and Nysha maam figured it out and asked, "What are you thinking? What is going on in your mind?"

"What about those people who are striving for basic necessities; that live below poverty line? Is GOD not merciful to them?"

"They are still grateful to GOD for they're not handicapped, they can still earn and eat; they are grateful that they get extra benefits like subsidy from the government, they are grateful that their husband or wife is still with them even in such poor conditions, they are grateful they are not suffering from any incurable disease; they also have end number of reasons to be grateful," Nysha maam explained and took her coffee and sipped.

"It's all the matter of thought. If you think positive, you'll have everything; and if you think negative, nothing seems good to you and you'll always feel deprived of one or the other thing," she said.

"Yes, you're right. I'd recently witnessed it in my life and I can see the change," Rajveer responded.

"Saying thank you is like a prayer to GOD and for that we need not to go to any temple, we can do it anywhere anytime and it's enough," Nysha maam stated.

I've got my prayer. From now I'll daily say thanks to GOD for everything He'd given to me let it be food, shelter, clothes, education, money, friends, scooty, nail polish, branded watches, perfumes, a visit to Goa, my ability to speak and write, for my healthy body, my beautiful surrounding, my thought process and everything, and of course thank you Nysha maam. My mind was saying.

All three had finished their coffee.

"Now I think I should take a leave," Nysha maam said.

"Nysha Ji wait for some more time, is there any urgency to go early?" Rajveer's mother said.

"No aunti, I've to reach home, it's already 7:00 pm."

"It's ok mom, don't force her, she has to go home," Rajveer said.

"Ok beta Ok," Rajveer's mother said to her son. All of them stood up and Rajveer's mother turned towards Nysha maam, hold her hands and said, "Thank you so much for coming here and making this idiot son of mine a well grown and matured boy."

That's my pleasure but I must say he is really a good boy," Nysha maam said.

All of them giggled.

Rajveer and Nysha maam stepped outside the house and once again Nysha maam said, "I have one more thing to say to you Rajveer."

"Yes please tell me," he said.

"Don't complicate the things. Simplify as much as you can," she said.

Rajveer didn't understand why Nysha maam is saying all this.

"Your mind is filled with many unwanted thoughts, declutter them. And not only your mind, do simplify your actions, relationships, thoughts and everything," she simplified.

Both were standing near Nysha maam's car.

"Simplify in what sense?" Rajveer asked.

"Take chances, tell the truth, learn to say NO, spend your money on the things you love, say I love you to someone in your life, feel the true love, sing out loud, share somebody's pain, apologize, laugh when you fall, tell someone how much they mean to you, tell the idiot how he/she hurts you, abuse someone who deserves it, sit alone, watch the rain, laugh till your stomach pains, dance even if you are too bad at it, pose stupidly for photos, give someone a hug when they need it and make sure you get one when you do, be naughty like child, live it, love it because life is only once," Nysha maam clarified.

"That will be done Nysha Ji," Rajveer said with his thumbs up.

Nysha maam sat in the car and budged towards her home.

CHAPTER 11

Appreciate your Life

I'm sure you are aware of these two words. In your daily routine life, you must have heard someone saying "THANK YOU" to some another one at some point of time. While paying the bill at supermarket, we say Thank You to the attendant. While coming out of parlor, women say Thank You to the beautician. Actors while receiving award says thank you to Jury and the audience. While writing books, author conveys his thanks to the readers. Have you ever thought why do these people say thank you? What is the reason behind this? What is the miracle behind these two words that it brings smile on the person's face? What is the secret of saying thank you?

Saying "Thank You" means you are counting your blessings, noticing simple pleasures and acknowledging everything that you receive. Thank You means you are appreciating the people involved in your life who helped you to reach at this stage of your life where you stand now. Saying thank you can be a difficult thing for some people, while some people I know feels it a formality to say thank you to their near and dear ones. But doing so means admitting that you are in another's debt, it means you're admitting that another individual did something for you. After all human race is not all powerful, it is interdependent, one can't live life all alone, and we are constantly relying on each other for all kind of resources physically, financially and emotionally. And when you say thank you, it does mean that you acknowledge for what you've received and you're really grateful for it.

> *"If the only prayer you say in your life is*
> *"Thank You" that would suffice."*
> *—Meister Eckhart*

Gratitude shifts your focus from what your life lacks to the abundance that is already present. Giving thanks makes people happier and more resilient, it strengthens relationships, it improves health and it reduces stress. As Mother Teresa says "There is more hunger for love and appreciation in this world than for bread." There are end numbers of reasons for what you can be grateful for. You have eyes to see the beautiful world, a family to support you, your friends to help you, a job to earn money, a child to play with and many more. Take a few moments from our daily routine life and ponder on these questions, "What have I received from . . . . . . ?" "What have I given to . . . . ?" And "What trouble have I caused . . . ?" Acknowledge those who touched your life from the Barista who made your coffee to the engineers who drove your train and reflect upon how you have reciprocated your humbleness and gratefulness. Did you curse your train to come late or did you thank the driver to cover up the time and reached your station on time? Those who feel grateful have more energy, more optimism, more social connections and more happiness than those who do not. They are also less likely to be depressed, envious, greedy or alcoholics.

> *"You have it easily in your power to increase sum total of this world's happiness now. How? By giving a few words of appreciation to someone who is lonely or discouraged. Perhaps you will forget tomorrow the kind words you say today, but the recipient may cherish them over a lifetime."*
>
> —*Dale Carnegie*

❧ ❀ ❧

STORY: Whatever Happens With Us; Is Definitely GOOD For Us.

Once there was a small kid on earth. One fine day she came to know that god is distributing apples to humans in his place at heaven. The kid was so happy to receive that news and she went with lot of enjoyment to heaven to get the apple from god. There was a big queue standing to get apple from god and this kid also joined in that queue. While she was standing, she was fully excited and thrilled for the fact that she is going to receive in person from god's hands. Her turn too came and the kid showed her both the hands to receive apple. God gave the apple but unfortunately the tiny hands couldn't hold that big apple. Apple fell down and got wasted in mud. The kid got so disappointed. The ministers near the god informed that if the kid likes to have an apple from god again then she has to again follow the queue. Having waited for so long the kid didn't want to return back to earth with empty hands so she decided to wait again in the queue.

This time the queue has become even longer than the previous one. While waiting in queue, the kid could see lot of people who returns back with apple in hands and utmost satisfaction on their faces. The kid was so much disappointed and thought why me alone didn't get the apple in hand when all others were easily able to get it. What is the sin I did that I alone should suffer like this. Now the kid was so scared that she should not miss the apple again. Again her turn came and god gave the apple to the kid's hands and after giving the apple god spoke to the kid.

"My dear child, last time after giving you the apple only I noticed the apple I gave to you was a rotten apple and that's why I made that to fell down from your hands. Having given you a rotten apple, I felt bad for you and I wanted to give you the best apple in the farm and that time the best apple in the farm was growing and that's why I made you to wait such a long time in the queue.

Here it is. Now the apple that you have in hand is 'The Best' apple in the farm till to date. Enjoy."

MORAL: Friends, sometimes it so happens, as even after we put our 100% dedication and commitment things may get delayed or things may go wrong. Believe that god has something great for us and that's why this has happened. Always say, 'Gratitude & patience is absolutely the best way to bring more in one's life'

> *"If you count all your assets, you will always show a profit."*
> —*Robert Quillen*

Research Shows Gratitude Heightens Quality of Life

Two psychologists, Michael McCollough of Southern Methodist University in Dallas, Texas, and Robert Emmons of the University of California at Davis, wrote an article about an experiment they conducted on gratitude and its impact on well-being. The study split several hundred people into 3 different groups and all of the participants were asked to keep daily diaries. The first group kept a diary of all events that occurred during the day without being told specifically ti write about either good or bad things; the second group was told to record their unpleasant experiences; and the last group was instructed to make a daily list of things for which they were grateful. The results of the study indicated that daily gratitude exercises resulted in higher reported levels of alertness, enthusiasm, determination, optimism and energy. In addition, those in the gratitude group experienced less depression and stress, were more likely to help others, exercised more regularly, and made greater progress toward achieving personal goals. They tend to be more creative, bounce back more quickly more adversity.

Make a List

When you ask someone what they want, they start telling you about their lacking like, "I want a new car", "I want more money", "I want to go abroad" etc. Certainly there is nothing wrong in asking what you want but what is more important is to focus your mind from lacking to the abundance (what you already have). To try this take out a sheet of paper and start writing down what you want in your life, and your list might look like this:

1. A brand new car
2. A big house
3. Earn more money
4. To do a world tour
5. To loose some weight

Now take out another sheet of paper and start writing down your "BLESSINGS" means write about all those things that you already have and for which you are grateful, and now your list might look like this:

1. My family
2. My friends
3. My spouse / children
4. A job to earn livelihood
5. Roof over my head
6. Clothes in my closet

7. Filtered water to drink
8. Eating pizza sitting in McDonalds
9. My health
10. My computer
11. My old bike That took me to do great fun
12. Feeling connected to GOD
13. Last Diwali trip with family
14. A night out at hill station etc

The basic idea behind doing all this is to be aware of your Blessings. Anytime you feel that you're completely lost and now you've nothing to do, take out your Blessings list and review it and feel grateful for what all you have. And when you focus on what you have, you live in a new world of creation and fun because when your thoughts, feelings, emotions and actions radiate unconditional love and gratitude, you create more and more abundance and gradually you'll find that the list of what you want is to be added in your blessings list.

"He is a wise man who does not grieve for the things which he has not, but rejoices for those which he has."

—Epictetus

"I have never been a millionaire. But I have enjoyed a great meal, a crackling fire, a glorious sunset, a walk with a friend, a hug from a child, a cup of soup, a kiss behind the car. There are plenty of life's tiny delights for all of us."

—Jack Anthony

Appreciate Life's Annoying Little Things

Do you know there were thousands of people who died during 9/11 attack on twin towers and still there were many people who escaped the bitter end of 9/11 attack and were able to live their life?

- There was a woman who was late because her alarm clock didn't go off in time
- One of them missed his bus
- One spilled food on her clothes and had to take time to change
- One's car wouldn't start
- One went back to answer the telephone
- One couldn't get a taxi
- One had a child who didn't get ready for school as he should have

So now whenever you're stuck in traffic, miss an elevator, turn back to answer a ringing telephone, all the little things that annoy you . . . . . Just think that this is exactly where GOD wants you to be at this very moment. The next time your morning seems to be going wrong, children are getting dressed slowly, you cant seen to find the car keys, don't get mad and frustrated, and don't panic. GOD is at work watching over you. So the next time when you see something or feel for something happening around you, always say thanks. Say thanks . . . .

- For the husband who is on the sofa being a couch potato because he is at home with you and not in the bars.

- For the taxes that you pay because it means that you're employed.
- For the mess to clean after a party because it means that you have been surrounded by friends.
- For your shadow that watches you work because it means that you're in sunshine.
- For a lawn that needs mowing, windows that need cleaning, and gutters that need fixing because it means you have a home.
- For the unwanted sound of horns because it means that you can hear.
- For the pile of laundry and ironing because it means you've clothes to wear.
- For weariness and aching of muscles at the end of the day because it means you have been capable of working hard.
- Finally, for too much email, because it means you have friends who are thinking of you.

"We have no right to ask when a sorrow comes, "Why did this happen to me?" unless we ask the same question for every joy that comes our way."

—Unknown

Some Techniques to be Grateful

1. Keep a gratitude journal: Note 1-3 good things that happened during the day and be specific.

2. Write a gratitude letter: To a person who has exerted a positive influence in your life but

to whom you've able to say or express your gratefulness.

3. Go on a gratitude visit: Meet a person who had helped you in your past and played a vital role in your life/career and say thanks to him/her face to face.

4. Savor good times: Collect photographs, drawings, cards which reinforce your good memories. Collect them in scrapbooks or post around your home.

5. Pause Mindfully: During a day, stop for a moment and focus on the sounds, smells and touch around you and feel them within you.

6. Count blessings, not sleep: If you're not feeling sleepy, don't count the stars or sheep's, start counting your blessing list, review people and events to be grateful for during your entire day before falling asleep.

Make gratitude—the canvas of your life over which good memories of events and people in your life is painted and keep this canvas in front of your eyes and daily watch it before sleeping in night or after waking up in the morning.

> *"God gave you a gift of 86,400 seconds today. Have you used one to say thank you?"*
>
> *—William Arthur Ward*

CHAPTER 12

Simplify Your Life

"When you learn how to say yes to the things you want in your life and no to the things you don't want in your life—your life becomes simpler."

—Unknown

A simple life has different meaning and a different value for every person. For me it means living the life I want, indulge in the tasks I love to do, spend my time with my loved ones and live in peace without any hectic schedule and chaos. A simple life means getting to understand what's important to you and eliminating the rest from your life. It seems simple in reading but the problem is most of the people didn't even know what's important to them. There are some people who know what they want and still there are many more people who just walk along with the crowd.

There are many examples of simplifying your life, your relationships, your actions, your thoughts, your daily routine life and all other stuff. It's not necessary that each and every example will work for you. This is your task to identify—does this example is for me. Can I simplify my life just by adopting such certain things which are so easy and relevant? You have to choose the ones that appeal and apply to your life.

Simplify Your Life

- Start everyday with your most important task, leaving other ones undone.
- Do what you said you will do first.
- Learn to say No.
- Ask others for help whenever you need it.
- Finish things completely, don't leave it only to have to come back again and again.
- Pick one thing at a time to do and focus on it.
- Leave spare time for yourself unscheduled and uncommitted.
- Prioritize your to do list.
- Keep one to do list and keep it short (only the most important things should be on it at any time).
- Take time to be in solitude.
- Take time to pray and meditate.
- Find and eliminate other wasteful actions in your life.
- Read every single day.
- Plan your week and all major tasks for that week.
- Review your accomplishments each week.
- Be grateful for what you have, what you can do, and for everything in your life.

- Turn off your cell phone for sometime and be with yourself.
- Eat simple meals and don't cook things that don't need to be cooked.
- Automate any bills, payments, and money transactions that you can.
- Ignore distractions from media.
- Commute by bicycle or public transit instead of the busy freeway.
- Use commuting time wisely by reading or listening to books.
- Consider a career or job change to reduce stress.
- Get rid of clothes you no longer wear or have worn in 6 months.
- Sell or give away household items you rarely / never use.
- Eliminate two things for every one new thing you acquire.
- Lend things out to friends often and don't ask for it back if you don't need it.
- Buy less stuff by only buying basic needs.
- Move to a smaller house or living space and get rid of all extra stuff.
- Give away books when you are done with them and let someone else enjoy them.
- Engage in simple hobbies that don't require a lot of stuff (music, art, writing).
- Consider going greener since this requires reducing things that consume power / energy.
- Get rid of your televisions or at least reduce the time you spend watching.
- Don't carry all your credit or debit cards, just a small amount of cash for emergency.

- Downsize your vehicles or sell one.
- Clear out all clutter and extra stuff from your vehicle.
- Spend the weekend with friends and family.
- Have a place for everything and keep it organized in place.
- Label, simplify and organize your file systems (both physical and electronic).
- Consolidate your email accounts, bank accounts and others.
- Recycle and reuse as much as possible.
- Give to those who have less than you.
- Volunteer your time for service to others.
- Keep a vegetable garden.
- Grow some plants and flowers.
- Enjoy nature's company.
- Be honest with others (it will help avoid complex issues and conflict).
- Treat everyone with respect, not just your close friends or relationship.
- Treat everyone fairly; don't complicate things with favoritism.
- Accept people for who they are and don't expect them to change.
- Compare yourself only to yourself from the past, no one else.
- Ask your friends and family for things they are looking for, and give them any items you can do.
- Keep all your contacts and address book items in one place.
- Involve your whole family with simplifying your life.
- Tell your friends about what you want to achieve by simplifying.

- Pick some of the actions above and do them with a friend.
- Focus on activities for doing things instead of buying.
- Spend less time with the "negatrons" around you and more time with positive people.
- Apologize quickly for any hurtful actions.
- Spend time in private with a significant other each week.
- Go for walks and have time to just talk with your friends and family (you don't always need to be doing anything).
- Make a gift for someone else instead of buying one.
- Write a personal thank you note or letter to a friend.
- Call someone you care for with no reason other than to tell them you were thinking of them and wish them a wonderful day.
- Walk away from all gossip and don't participate in those conversations.
- Put family meals at home first and don't let work get in the way.
- Stay completely disconnected from work on weekends and vacations.
- Listen to others and stop talking so much about yourself.
- Be contented with life for health, love and happiness instead of with belongings.
- Keep less goals and plans (focus on just 2 or 3 at a time).
- Exercise often as this clears the mind and keeps you healthy longer through life.

- Make time to do what you love and to provide relief from stress.
- Make a list of all your simple pleasures in life and pick an item from it to do every day.
- Evaluate new things by asking "Will this help to simplify my life?"
- Let go of perfectionism.
- Find what calms you and visualize it to reduce stress.
- Be positive and look for the best in things.
- Be anxious for nothing and live more in the moment.
- Let go of things from the past.
- Face and get over your fears.
- Always look for ways to improve one self.
- Express gratitude.
- Know and stick to your limits for commitments.
- Seek knowledge only to apply it as wisdom.
- Look for and express love to yourself and others.
- Choose to be happy and at peace with yourself.
- All that you express will come back to you so, think and express what you want for yourself.
- Seek and love God and He will provide, you need not worry about anything else.
- Everything is okay in the end. If it's not okay, then it's not the end.
- Throw out nonessential numbers. This includes age, weight and height. Let the doctor worry about them. That is why you pay him/her.
- Keep only cheerful friends. The grouches pull you down.
- Keep learning. Learn more about the computer, crafts, gardening, whatever.

- Never let the brain idle. "An idle mind is the devil's workshop" And the devil's name is Alzheimer's.
- Enjoy the simple things.
- Laugh often, long and loud. Laugh until you gasp for breath.
- The tears happen. Endure, grieve, and move on. The only person, who is with us our entire life, is ourselves. Be ALIVE while you are alive.
- Surround yourself with what you love, whether it's family, pets, keepsakes, music, plants, and hobbies, whatever. Your home is your refuge.
- Cherish your health: If it is good, preserve it. If it is unstable, improve it. If it is beyond what you can improve, get help.
- Don't take guilt trips. Take a trip to the mall, to the next county, to a foreign country, but NOT to where the guilt is.
- Tell the people you love that you love them, at every opportunity.
- Get rid of (or at least reduce) commitments that you do out of obligation.
- Add items you want to a wish list as you think of them.
- Make time to catch up with an old friend.
- Ask for experiences not things for your birthday and Christmas this year.
- Tell the truth.
- Consolidate debt.
- Keep a bag for garbage in your car.
- Cary a notebook and pen with you where ever you go.
- Enjoy the present moment as much as you can.
- Take time to really see the little things in life.

- Reduce the amount of TV you watch.
- Get outside.
- Create morning, daytime, and evening routines.
- Don't get caught up in other people's drama.
- Let go of the self-imposed need to be perfect.
- Focus on a simple, but healthy, eating plan.
- Share responsibilities.
- Reduce your wardrobe to a few versatile items.
- Start a gratitude journal.
- Finish old tasks before taking on new ones.
- Focus on one thing at a time.
- Take time to relax and unwind. Find something relaxing to do. It doesn't matter what it is, a bubble bath, a massage or just quietly reading a book, give yourself this important time.
- Get plenty of sleep.
- Take a deep breath.
- Take short breaks at work.
- Have fun like a child.
- Express yourself.
- Listen to your body, listen to your instincts and listen to others.
- Be kind.
- Give genuine compliments and share a smile!

Ultimately there is just one thing to remember, this life is yours. Take the power to choose what you want to do and do it well. Take the power to love what you want in life and love it honestly. Take the power to control your own life. No one else can do it for you. Take the power to live your life happily.

9th Meeting

Rajveer stepped out from his car. He was wearing light blue coloured jeans with purple coloured t-shirt marked GAP on it. He kept his car keys in his pocket and started walking towards the top of a small mountain.

After 5 minutes of walk, he saw Nysha maam standing, with her face towards the open sky. She was wearing pink and green coloured kurta and her hands were on the fencing placed all around the border of top of mountain.

Rajveer figured out Nysha maam satnding over there and moved towards her.

The view of the place is awesome. Nyhsa maam was standing at the edge of the mountain. Standing there one can see wide open sky where sun is about to set; leaving behind only its rays to lighten up the sky with orange-red-yellow colour. Moving the eyes slowly downwards, one can see other small mountains covered by lot many trees.

Today there was not much crowd. There were only few people wherein one of the families was taking photographs with the sun in the hand and posing for different postures having sun in the frame.

"Good evening Nysha Ji," Rajveer said smiling and was standing behind her.

Nysha maam turned back to identify the voice and looking Rajveer she said, "Very good evening Rajveer."

"Right on time," Nysha maam tittered while looking her wrist watch.

"I always come on time," Rajveer said.

And both of them laughed louder this time.

"This place is amazing. I came here for the first time," said Rajveer.

"Yes it is, I just love this place," she said.

"How often do you come here?" Rajveer asked.

"Once in 2 months," she replied.

Rajveer nodded and was looking the sun setting down.

After sometime the crowd vanished and only both of them were there.

"I'd called you here for a purpose," Nysha maam said.

"Really? What purpose?" Rajveer asked.

"Rajveer this is echo point. You know what it means?" Nysha maam asked.

"Yes, whatever we speak out, it'll return back to us," Rajveer said simply.

"Yes, you are right. Similarly, our life, our universe, our surroundings, thoughts and actions too are just like echo point. Whatever we send to them, we'll get back the same," she mentioned.

"Let's try something. Say something loudly," Nysha maam said.

"What?"

"Say anything."

"I am the best," Rajveer shrieked aloud.

I am the best. I am the best. I am the best. I am the best. Same words were repeated at echo point.

"Say, I can do anything," she said.

"I can do it," Rajveer screamed with his mouth wide open towards the open sky.

I can do anything. I can do anything. I can do anything.

"Say, I am unique. I am nature's miracle."

He shouted again and it echoed back.

"Haah . . . . It feels great. So much energy is given to it and we get revitalized; isn't it?" Rajveer said looking into the eyes of Nysha maam.

"That's the beauty of this place," Nysha maam responded and looked at him.

"Rajveer, now you are endowed with a plate full of variety of food with daal, sabzi, roti, raita, mithai, papad, achaar etc but it's only you who have to take the pain of eating that food and fill your appetite," Nysha maam proclaimed.

"Yes, I understood Nysha Ji," he said.

"Now it's time to live again with a new vision, a new horizon and a new YOU," Nysha maam said.

Rajveer was listening carefully.

"And always remember these golden words; I can do it. Whenever you face a problem or in a critical situation or loose your confidence, say it to yourself, "I can do it, I am the best, I can do it." Nysha maam said.

"Yes now I can do it Nysha Ji. I promise one day I'll be back to you and you'll be amazed on what I've become," Rajveer said confidently.

OMG! What had happened to him today? He was so confident and this was the first time, I can see the glow in his eyes the same way I use to see in Nysha maam's eyes. I can't believe it's Rajveer who is saying all stuff like this; but I do believe that Nysha maam can do anything.

"There is no one in this world like you, since the inception of your birth none is similar to your eyes, your brain, your nose, hands, ears and hairs. No one has the same handwriting what you have, nobody behaves like you, there is no one who speaks the way you speak, and nobody has the same style as of yours. You are the one and only one. You are unique. So just be yourself and don't imitate others. You are here for a purpose, get to know about it and just do it," Nysha maam stated.

Rajveer was shaking his right hand with his tight fist and it seems as if he was repeating Nysha maam's words in his mind.

Today Rajveer's behaviour was quite different from the usual one.

Meanwhile the mobile rang. Tring tring.

"Yes mom," Rajveer said. "Yes yes I'll reach home within half an hour and I'll eat at home only," and hung up the phone.

"Your mom right?" Nysha maam said.

"Yes, now she uses to call me after every 2 hour and ask about me," he said and after a pause he continued, "I was so wrong; she actually loves me a lot. After such long time, I feel so good at my own home and this is all because of you Nysha Ji, thank you so much."

Rajveer almost sobbed.

Nysha maam hold his hands in her hands for few moments and said, "You deserve it Rajveer," patting his shoulder.

"I think you should take a leave now, your mom is waiting for you," she said.

"Yeah sure and are we meeting newt?" Rajveer asked.

"I'm done from my side Rajveer; my job is done. Now we don't have any more meetings," Nysha maam said politely.

"What? It's over now? Really? Are we done?" Rajveer said shockingly.

He almost reiterated these words 3 times.

"Yes Rajveer, it's done. Now it's up to you how you take it. Doctor's job is to give the prescription but you have to take the medicines regularly on your own. If you don't recover; surely you're not taking the medicines," she clarified.

"Although it's done but still we can meet," Rajveer said firmly.

"Now we'll meet only when you discover a new Rajveer within you; and I'm sure you can do it. You'll eventually get to know about it through your surroundings, your results, your relationships. And when you discover it yourself; that day come and meet me. Now I want a transformed Rajveer," Nysha maam said in a tone listening to which one can be motivated strong enough to prove himself.

Rajveer nodded half-heartedly.

Half heartedly because she likes Nysha maam and it's because of her that he is getting a new life and now he'll not be able to meet her for long time until he becomes the one she wants.

Both of them started moving toward their car.

Rajveer escorted Nysha maam to her car. Nysha maam sat inside waved to him and within a minute her car was out of sight.

And Rajveer was standing all alone and the only voice that can be heard was of Nysha maam that was wandering in Rajveer's mind.

CHAPTER 13

I Can Do It

"I'm only one, but still I'm one. I cannot do everything, but still I can do something, and because I cannot do everything, I will not refuse to do something that I can do."
—*Hellen Keller*

1. I can't loose my weight.
2. I can't marry the girl I love.
3. I'm not able to get promotion this year.
4. I think the baby can't be saved.
5. I can't earn more than Rs.20000 p.m.
6. I can't buy that luxurious car.
7. I'm not so rich to do world tour.
8. I don't think that my dream will be ever fulfilled.
9. I can't reach to the sales targets.
10. I won't be able to get 90% marks this year.
11. I'm too old to continue study. I can't pursue it.
12. I can't swim, I'm, too fat.
13. I can't pay the EMI's.
14. I can't run in a marathon.

15. Finding life on moon is impossible.
16. Getting g a job in NASA will always be a dream.
17. I don't have time to attend your party.
18. I can't speak in public.
19. I can't concentrate on my work.

These are some of the general statements we often hear from one or the other in our daily routine life. Everybody is puzzled in one or the other thing; nobody is satisfied from what one has and always feels greedy for the things on the other side. What they already have doesn't value to them much and what they actually want, they give just simple excuses like, "I can't", "It's impossible", It's not in my hands", "This is out of my limit" and so on.

To accomplish the most difficult tasks, you need to put in a lot of hard work, extra perseverance and concentration on a single objective. You should have patience and faith in yourself. You should have determination, dedication and devotion to attain success. Never bother about the results. Keep on going even if the pace is slow; just ensure that it remains steady. Whenever your mind focus on "I can't", immediately control your mind and switch it to the "I can" mode. There is no such task in the world which is impossible.

Earlier people use to gaze at moon and say, "What if we have the life on moon also." That time it was just a statement but now it's a reality. Scientists are doing every research to get the life on moon. Earlier people can only dream of flying like a bird in the open sky but today it's a reality. What was impossible at that time; is a reality now. Earlier people don't have laptops, no connectivity, and now one person is just one second away to connect to other person. Today and even yesterday also everything was possible. Its just we need a thought in mind to achieve and concentrate fully over it to get it done. No task is impossible. Everything is possible and you can do everything, you just get to know how your goal can be achieved. As Charles Swindoll says, "If you're running a 26 mile marathon, remember that every mile you run is one step at a time. If you are writing a book, do it one page at a time. If you're trying to master a new language, try it one word at a time. There are 365 days in an average year. Divide any project by 365 and you'll find that no job is all that intimidating."

To attain your desired goal, don't get worried when you face trouble instead laugh at it and forget it. When you laugh at your trouble, you'll find it to be mere bubble which is swiftly blown away. To gather the fruit, to register victory, to score success, you require unwavering faith in yourself. A person who trusts himself is an optimist. Some one has said, "Two men look out through the same bars; one sees the mud and the other sees the stars." An optimist sees an opportunity in every calamity. If you worry and despair about impossibilities they will simply multiply. Never let your mind think that any task is impossible. Always endeavor with new zeal and say, "Yes, I can do it." Your attitude should be right. With a resolute, positive and committed attitude you can invariably develop the right aptitude. That is why Dr. Karl Meninger had stated, "Attitudes are more important than facts." By changing your negative attitude, you can shed your tormenting fears, doubts, despair an inferiority complex.

> **"Don't let what you cannot do interfere with what you can do."**
> **—John Wooden**

> **"Ability is what you're capable of doing. Motivation determines what you do. Attitude determines how well you do it."**
> **—Lou Holtz**

In the movie Black, Rani Mukherjee had played the role of a blind girl; and by her own efforts, dedication and determination she gets graduation degree at the age of 40. Had she given up in between? No. She believed in herself that she can do it and she tried for it continuously until she got it. If you can persuade yourself that you can do certain thing; you will do it; no matter how difficult it is.

President of United States Barack Obama was criticized that he is not experienced when he ran for the presidency and the same thing happen when Bill Gates stood up for presidency. Many proved that nothing is impossible and if you really want something, you can achieve it. You might not have the privileged background; you might have neglected all your education so far and even then, if you realize your mistakes and work for the betterment of studies, profession and your life then you can definitely achieve the results. Examples are plenty, Dr. APJ Abdul Kalam has come from rural background, studied in government schools and only with hard work and dedication he has achieved so many things and he had inspired many others in the world. Steve Jobs could not afford a good meal while he was in college but later he was founder of Apple and set a new history. Others are J.K.Rowling, Mahatma Gandhi, Bill Gates, and Stephen Hawking etc. So pack your problems and worries into a bag and move forward.

> *"If I have the belief that I can do it, I shall surely acquire the capacity to do it even if I may not have it at the beginning."*
> —*Mahatma Gandhi*

STORY: Bruce Lee

"Bruce had me up to three miles a day, really at a good pace. We'd run the three miles in twenty-one or twenty-two minutes. Just under eight minutes a mile[Note: when running on his own in 1968, Lee would get his time down to six-and-a half minutes per mile].

So this morning he said to me "We're going to go five." I said, "Bruce, I can't go five. I'm a eluvia lot older than you are, and I can't do five." He said, "When we get to three, we'll shift gears and it's only two more and you'll do it."

I said "Okay, hell, I'll go for it." So we get to three, we go into the fourth mile and I'm okay for three or four minutes, and then I really begin to give out. I'm tired, my heart's pounding, I can't go any more and so I say to him, "Bruce if I run any more,"—and we're still running-" if I run any more I'm liable to have a heart attack and die."

He said, "Then die." It made me so mad that I went the full five miles.

Afterward I went to the shower and then I wanted to talk to him about it. I said, you know, "Why did you say that?"

He said, "Because you might as well be dead. Seriously, if you always put limits on what you can do, physical or anything else, it'll spread over into the rest of your life. It'll spread into your work, into your morality, into your entire being. There are no limits. There are plateaus, but you must not stay there, you must go beyond them. If it kills you, it kills you. A man must constantly exceed his level."

From The Art of Expressing the Human Body
By Bruce Lee, John Lit

So the next time you fail in achieving your goal, just stand up, brush yourself, fill yourself with all positive energy and keep moving towards your goal. Even when its hard to move, take small steps forward; because every step will lead you farther away from where you were yesterday. Whatever you wish can be achieved. You are the Gennie of your life. It's never too late to be what you always wanted to be. You are never too old to set another goal and you are never so weak to achieve your goal. So if all big leaders and achievers can do it; why can't you???

6 Years Later

Ting tong. Ting tong.

After few seconds the gate opened.

A very beautiful lady opened the door. She was in her 40's but was looking younger than before. She was wearing green red and white salwar kurta. Her hairs were clutched this time able to make a juda. I guess her hairs are long now. To be clutched together at one knot. She was wearing small diamond ear rings which were sparkling in the light.

"Rajveer? Alisha? What a surprise? How are you? It's been such a long time and how come you both are here?" the lady thrown so many questions to be answered. She was half happy and half surprised.

"Good evening Nysha Ji," Rajveer greeted while bowing down his head in front of her.

Yes the lady is Nysha maam.

"Good evening maam," Alisha greeted and touched her feet.

Hii this is me Alisha Ranawat; wife of Rajveer Ranawat.

"Nysha Ji, can we come in?" Rajveer giggled.

"Oh yes yes please come in. Come Alisha, I still can't believe you both are here," Nysha maam hold my hands and asked us to come inside but she was still in shock.

All three of us entered.

Near the entrance gate there was a beautiful vase filled with fresh red and yellow roses and its fragrance can still be felt in the hall. Towards the left there was sofa set with a center table. In one extreme corner there was placed a 40" LED TV beside which there was a big window through which one can see the kids playing in the society ground.

"Come have a seat," Nysha maam said.

All three of us settled down. I and Nysha maam sat close to each other and Rajveer faced both of us.

"So Rajveer you look smarter than before and what happened to your body. Have you done some surgery or what? You look like a bollywood hero," Nysha maam said to Rajveer and was smiling.

Yes Rajveer looked smarter than before. He was exactly looking like those models featured in the big hoardings and banners. His biceps were attractive and bold enough. Perfect lean body shaped; a perfect physique.

Her smile was the sign that she was very happy today to see both of us after a long time.

The maid came in with 3 glasses of water and kept them carefully on the table.

"Thank you Nysha Ji, but it isn't any miracle or magic of surgery. It's my passion," Rajveer replied.

"Passion?" Nysha maam looked puzzled.

I took my glass of water and drank it.

"You remember Nysha Ji, I'd told you about my passion and that's gyming and exercising. Now I knew that it was my passion and I'd involved myself into it which resulted into this physique but I'm grateful to my better half Alisha that she had a perfect plan for me to convert my passion into money making, a new business venture for me," Rajveer explained.

Nysha maam looked at me and smiled. And both of them took their glass of water and drank it.

"Business?" Nysha maam said.

"Yes business Nysah Ji. By GOD's grace now I've 8 branches of my "Fit n Fine" gym in India and Dubai with a base of 350 customers and everything is going all fantastic," Rajveer replied.

"That's really great. I'm proud of you Rajveer," Nysha maam said.

"And what about me?" I asked like a child to her.

"Oh Alisha, you're darling, you are a gem," Nysha maam said and then asked, "And what are you doing these days Alisha?"

"Maam I've completed my PhD degree in Psychology and right now I'm on a research on human behavioural aspects at Delhi University," I said.

"That's wonderful," Nysha maam said.

"But I wonder how come you both . . . . . I mean Rajveer, when does this happen? When were you both married? What's the story all about?" Nysha maam asked and she further filled the hall with more questions, "And Alisha you, how come you fell in love with him. I mean you were with me all the time. My mind is totally confused. You both didn't tell me about it."

The maid came in again and this time with a tray full of snacks, cold drinks and some sweets including kaju barfi and rasgulla (my favourite).

"Nysha Ji I didn't told you about this because till that time I was not fully polished and I'd promised to myself That I'll meet you only when I'll become the diamond of your choice," Rajveer said.

Listening to his words, Nysha maam's eyes filled with tears but before it can come out, she stopped them there itself with her dupatta.

There are 2 types of women in this world. One who stop their tears at the edge of eyes only and the other who can fill the buckets of tears and one can use that water for gardening. The first one is decent, emotional yet practical and understanding woman and the second one is typical Indian woman who cries only to get what she wants.

"She was with you all the time, that's why she knows me better; even better than myself," Rajveer said cheerfully.

Yes I was with Nysh maam for 1 whole year as a trainee/assistant. I was getting trained under her direction for my further studies in psychology. I used to sit in her office on the right side of her office gate. Sitting there I can see the broad view of sky through the big glass window which was right in front of me.

After 2 months of my joining, Rajveer came and meet Nysha maam and that day for the first time I saw Rajveer.

"So you both were mingling from that time hmmm," Nysha maam scoffed.

"Oh no maam, we didn't even talked for 2 years," I interrupted.

"What? Then when did you meet?" Nysha maam asked.

"Actually Nysha Ji, after our session was over, I was indulged totally on how to discover the diamond and one day I just went to a mall in a concert where I met Alisha. She came there with her friends. We both recognized each other and had casual talks and I asked her about you and she said that her training was over so she left from there and was now doing her PG in psychology and that was the first day I actually talked with her," Rajveer said.

I was nodding my head in approval as to what he was saying was right.

Nysha maam was listening carefully to him and from inside she was quite excited too.

He further continued, "Then we exchanged our numbers and have casual chats. Well she knew everything about me as she was with you and was also studying my case. So that was the plus point for me. Meanwhile she supported me a lot both emotionally and spiritually to rediscover a new Rajveer within me. I must say you'd given her good training and she is a good student that she had imbibed your qualities."

All of us laughed and paused to have a snacks break but Nysha maam was very eager to know more so she said, "Rajveer you can eat the whole snacks but do continue your story too," and she smiled.

Afetr so long time I was seeing Nysha maam smiling. I really missed her smile.

"And then she'd helped me to start the business so she had the plan, I had contacts and met Neeraj regarding this, got loan from the bank, love from my mother, wishes from GOD, aspiring soul from within which you had inserted in me and that's it; when all of these were mixed in a blender, you get this Rajveer," he said.

"And today I have chains of my gym in Delhi, Mumbai, Chandigarh, Pune, Bangalore, Baroda, Dubai and Nepal," he said.

"That's really great Rajveer, in short span of 6 years you achieved a lot and I see in your eyes that you are very happy," Nysha maam said.

"Yes I'm very happy and there is a saying that behind every successful man there is a woman but I've 3 women in my life; you, my mother and my beloved wife. Thanks to all 3 of you," he said and took up the glass of cold drink high enough and cheers in the air.

We both also took up our glasses and said cheers.

Rajveer has not finished yet and he continued, "I and Alisha met continuously for about one year and when I felt that she is one who will complete me, we got married," and thus Rajveer compiled his story.

And then suddenly a voice came in, "Mom where are you? I'm so hungry today," a sweet but loud voice came in.

A long height girl in her 20's came inside wearing white chudidaar and kurta with matching white flats. She had long, straight and silky hairs kind of those which are seen in shampoo ads. She was wearing lot of colourful bangles in her hands and to add her beauty she had dimples on both the cheeks.

She came inside excitedly but when she saw all of us, she tried to calm her and said, "Hi mom, hello bhaiya" and then she turned towards me and said, "Oh Alisha didi! Hi! How are you? Where were you for such long time? And look at you, you're looking so beautiful," she exclaimed.

She was also filled with excitement to see me and like her mother, she also had so many questions to ask but she was stopped by Nysha maam when she said, "Teena this is Rajveer bhaiya, your didi's husband and Rajveer this is Teena; my daughter."

"Hello Teena! How are you?" Rajveer said.

"I'm fine bhaiya," Teena said and sat beside me.

"Where are you coming from?" I asked Teena.

"I am coming back from dance classes" she made a typical hand gesture and said, "Classical dance."

"That's great. And how are your studies going on?" I asked again.

"Studies are too boring, I just hate that but for next year I'm planning for fashion designing," she replied.

"Well in that case you're like Rajveer bhaiya, he also didn't liked studies," Nysha maam said.

And all of us laughed.

"I just go and change and will be back in few minutes," Teena said and went inside.

"Alisha you haven't tasted rasgulla yet," Nysha maam said while offering the rasgulla plate to me.

I took one, gulped it and then I took another one. I feel no shame while eating and that to rasgulla; my favourite, no way.

Nysha maam and Rajveer looked at me and I was looking at rasgulla.

"So Rajveer, how is your mother now?" Nysha maam asked.

"She is fine. She lives with us and she is good," Rajveer replied.

"And your father?" Nysha maam asked.

As soon as Nysha maam asked this question, I looked at Rajveer and hold his hands. Whenever Rajveer is asked about his father, his face pales down and sometimes he get agitated. But today he tried to control his emotions and said in deep husky voice, "You remember you came at my home one day."

Nysha maam nodded.

He continued, "A week later my father came back from business tour and we'd a talk or rather argument, he was rigid and was still very rude to my mother. He didn't accept his mistake of beating my mother when I was not at home. He was not at all ashamed of his act but was standing still. We both, I and my mother ignored him for some more time but his drinking habit continued and one day I caught him red handed with another woman. I just hate him for this. I talked to him gave him another chance and like this some more weeks passed. But he was adamant, didn't change himself and was fully obsessed with that another woman. So finally I and my mother decided to leave him and we shifted to another place."

Rajveer's eyes become wet and sobbed but he has still somrthing more to say and he said, "I struggled a lot, almost went to every bank and suddenly I met Alisha and she supported me a lot and today I'm here."

"It's Ok Rajveer, forget about it. If a person is not ashamed or feel guilty of his mistake, leave him on his own. If your father would have changed, I'm sure you would have accepted him. You don't have to feel guilty of leaving your father. You had given him a chance but he didn't changed. It's really Ok, don't be upset," Nysha maam sympathized.

"I'm back now," Teena said and jumped to sit beside me.

She came back and looked fresh; I guess she'd a shower. She was wearing brown Capri and white top and she was looking pretty.

But still there was silence in the room but no longer when Teena said, "Why is everybody quite?"

And all of us just smiled.

And then Teena said to me, "Alisha didi, have some rasgulla" offering the plate.

Rajveer and Nysha maam looked at me but I ignored them and took one rasgulla and ate it.

And then we had lot many chats with some more rasgullas which continued till late evening.

Now Your Turn

Do you feel your life lacks enthusiasm and accomplishment? Do you find every year the same as it was the last year? Do you feel that your promises are not fulfilling? Are you satisfied with your life at this very moment? Do you feel you have everything you dreamt of? Would you like to learn to create a life that directly reflects your talents and interests? Are you ready to know yourself?

To answer all your questions, take out some time and fill this questionnaire. The following will help you to identify yourself, your likes, dislikes, values and it will cover all aspects of your life.

You have to answer the questions as to on what degree you follow them. Read the questions one by one and tick marks your answer of frequency in the given column. Do it for all the questions and at last total your answers based on the based given below.

Always: 5
Very Often: 4
Sometimes: 3
Rarely: 2
Never: 1

Statements	Always	Very Often	Sometimes	Rarely	Never
1. I start my day with a smile.					
2. If I fail in doing something; I try it again.					
3. I plan my schedule for the day.					
4. I seek motivation from others or I am self motivated. (write one)					
5. I feel good about my current position/job/ situation of my life.					
6. I think about my dreams and get excited.					
7. I appreciate the things I like.					
8. I do physical, mental or spiritual exercise.					
9. I feel good about my relations with friends, family and relatives.					
10. I say "Thank You" whenever my work is done.					
11. I get the feeling of "I can't do it."					
12. I read self help books.					

13. I spend some time with nature.					
14. I leave my work pending to be done on the next day.					
15. I say "I love you" to myself looking into the mirror.					
16. I listen to the people around me and give them a chance to share their views.					
17. I care for the people around me.					
18. I am eager to learn new things.					
19. I welcome the criticism.					
20. I accept the change coming in my way.					
21. I share my dreams with others.					
22. My life is influenced by money.					
23. I visualize the things before doing it.					
24. I get along with others easily.					
25. I think positive in the time of challenges.					

Excellent (105-125): Wonderful. You get things done and you don't let anything stand your way. You make a conscious effort to stay self motivated and you spend significant time and effort on setting goals and acting to achieve those goals. You attract and inspire others with your success. Treasure this and be aware that not everyone is as self motivated as you are.

Strong (85-105): Good. Keep it up. You are generally confident about yourself and your abilities. You are perfectly moving on your way. Move ahead and also take others and inspire them too.

Mediocre (65-85): You are doing OK on self motivation. You're certainly not falling; however you could achieve much more. To achieve what you want, try to increase the motivation factors in all areas of your life.

Poor (45-65): You allow your personal doubts and fears to keep you away from succeeding. You've probably had a few incomplete goals in the past, so you may have convinced yourself that you're not self motivated and then you've made that come true. Break this harmful pattern now and start believing in yourself again.

Negative (25-45): Negative self esteem. You are living in a negative atmosphere. You have little or no confidence in your abilities. You tend to demonstrate negative attitude.